The Points of Light

Book 7 in the Ongoing Desert Store Series

by Patsy Stanley

This is a Blue Watercress Ink Publication

ISBN 979-899-86104-5-5

There comes a Time when the Light must rise—and when it does, it doesn't call only the mighty. It calls the odd, the broken, and the ordinary souls who carry unexpected gifts. In the following story, the desert store misfits answered the call.

Avery, the quiet keeper of the desert store built on sacred ground, was gone. Something was shifting, going wrong. The rest of the psychic misfits knew it. There were over twenty of them...all psychic in their own ways, all connected with each other. William, observing and measuring from a distance. Lily, searching maps for more sacred energy sites like the desert store. Normaine, Native American and dapper Italian truck driver Eddy from New York. Timmon, the lost golden child, with his acute sense of smell, Louise Hope Cornfield, southern healer, and suave Gordon Tappenhouse Smythe, Teacher, Magician and Mime.

Others came just in time to join them. Shem, a waterman, walking the old path in the east, finding Miz Wind and Marisong. Beck, Tree Whisperer, and Hattie, House Whisperer, holding the line in western California with forest and house. Susan Sugar Diamond, famous orphan and author and her sidekick Lana, Matthew and Perry, Avery's blustery father and quiet brother, were together and on the move without knowing why. In Carolina, Geena and Celia wake at night to the sound of a woman's voice, calling to them from the sea. It was time to go. The misfits were to fight in the upcoming battle between

Good and Evil that the sacred ground the desert store stood on would be a part of.

Justice doesn't always wear a crown. It shows up in dented pickup trucks, cracked voices, and hands that have seen hard work. The people you'll meet in this story don't look like heroes. They're quirky, sometimes off-the-wall, with too human faults-but when the call came, they answered it. They took their strange, everyday skills—and lifted them to the sacred. Each character in this story carries a gift—a skill, a way of seeing or doing things. Some of these gifts are peculiar, like Crazy Jack's talent for filibustering, but all of them matter.

This is a story about justice, about Light, and about the people who dare to show up and fight for it in their own strange and beautiful ways.

You might not expect these characters to be heroes. That's the point. Read on, and see how Light moves through misfits and unlikely souls. You might just recognize a piece of yourself in them.

Table of Contents

Chapter One: The Veil Thins

Gonna' go there

Gonna' find out what's fair

and make my declare

Emma Makepeace was building a new life in Spain with a handsome, fine new husband. But ghosts don't care where you live. They'll find you. Especially ghosts with ominous messages that disturb your dreams.

William, Emma's father was a quiet warrior, silver-haired, soft-spoken. He was long, lanky, and lean, with a slow, easy grace that made people feel safe just by being near him.

In Emma's dreams, William had lost someone and it was fast becoming a life or death matter to find them.

Small and quiet and beautiful, Emma looked like a fragile bird perched on a fence wire. But looks were deceiving. Beneath her calm exterior lived a warrior, and unlike William, she had a hidden passionate side that warred constantly within her. A world-renowned artist, her expensive canvases were bold with wild splashes of color—defiant, alive, and enormous. That, and the secret locked room filled with thousands of romance novels, helped keep her passionate nature in check.

Over time, more ghosts began haunting her dreams. The misfits from the Desert Store-Normaine and Eddy, Mama and Geena and Celia, the three Mafia sisters, Timmon, and others-Matthew, Perry, Susan Sugar Diamond, Lana. All of them beckoned to her, speaking words of doom and gloom and eventually cussing plentifully at her because she didn't get a move on.

Then the three Magi- odd men- Bud, Ben, and Andy, who she had done paintings of setting them free from their ills- she never painted people! It happened as though she'd been called to help them- showed up in her dreams and cried, wringing their hands over her tardiness in not getting a move on.

"Okay. Enough!" She muttered in her sleep. Alexander, Emma's gentle, distinguished new husband, watched Emma's unrest. His concern grew with each passing day. He offered to go to America with her, but Emma knew this was a journey she had to take alone.

It was time to go back to the desert store. She made her decision in the quiet of the early morning, when the first light of dawn was just beginning to creep over the horizon. She would fly back to America, to the desert store and to William, to the place her heart had never truly left.

Though she loved Alexander deeply, somehow there was a battle coming involving her and her father, the store rats and others. She made flight plans. William needed her. So did the other misfits. She didn't know what she could do to help, but her love for them took her back home. The flight back to America took hours, but Emma wasn't in a hurry any more. No ghosts came to haunt her sleep on the flight...

William was thinking about Avery Mott Judson, his best friend. He'd been the owner of the Desert Store before his untimely death out back of it from a heart attack, and the hasty cremation of his remains that quickly followed. Something about the way Avery died had never set right with him. He'd gone over the quickness of his death in his mind countless times, knowing something was off, but he couldn't quite put his finger on it. Years passed, but the nagging feeling never completely left him, though he managed to settle into an uneasy acceptance of Avery's odd and abrupt end. But deep down, he knew that evil had struck Avery down, murdered him, and he, William, Avery's best friend, had somehow missed it.

Something was nagging at his mind, keeping him uneasy. It started a few weeks ago, subtle at first, like the faint shifting of a shadow in a corner of his mind, walking out into the Light, now it was becoming a clanging bell, keeping the sleeping warrior in his soul—a part of him he rarely let anyone see- wide awake.

Though he was known for his easygoing nature, his gentle demeanor, and his mild, unassuming way of moving through life, William had a steel core beneath it all. And that steel was thrumming again, vibrating with the undeniable feeling that something wasn't over. Something—or someone—was calling on him to act soon.

He sat back in his beach chair and closed his eyes. Long, lanky, blue jeaned with sky blue eyes, white hair pulled back into a braid, he hadn't cut his hair since Avery died. It was almost down to his waist. He didn't notice sounds or waves: he was too busy organizing memories of his and Avery's lives together.

Avery Mott Judson had been the youngest son of Matthew Judson, a millionaire entrepreneur. Perry, Avery's brother, was seven years older.

Avery grew up a lonely rich boy, surrounded by wealth but emotionally abandoned. His mother left Matthew, married a Duke in England, started a new life when Avery was three and Perry was ten. She ignored her two sons entirely, severing ties, adding another layer of rejection to Avery's life.

The brothers liked each other well enough in their own way. But Perry was often away somewhere, sent there by the latest "love" in his father's life.

After his first wife divorced him, Matthew quickly developed a tendency to marry his "latest love" and spoil her children, ignoring his own children.

He reasoned that if he paid attention to his boys, he would have to think about his first wife, their mother, who had left him, and he refused to do that. "They are like their mother," Matthew often said, and turned away from them. Because of this, Avery's childhood was marked by both luxury and profound loneliness.

When Avery was ten, tragedy struck. His father's latest wife Dawn had two daughters approaching puberty, and an eight year old son. Her two spoiled daughters drowned their brother in Matthew's private lake, and accused Avery of doing it.

Matthew, quick to placate Dawn and her daughters in their noisy grieving, hastily sent Avery to boarding school in Switzerland to avoid murder charges. Furious, Matthew ordered him to not come home ever again. Matthew believed he had drowned the boy out of jealousy.

Avery met William Makepeace at boarding school, and they forged a lifelong friendship. When their school days were over, they deliberately dropped out of sight. Their families didn't care where they were. As long as they didn't pester them, they were given plenty of money.

The two of them set off to see the world, searching for something their souls needed. They traveled to India to learn more about their spiritual natures. They traveled to Tibet and other sacred spiritual places, then to Spain, where Avery fell in love and learned about physical affection and how love can be given freely. He laughed and gloried in the tenderness of it with a lovely girl, and the old bitterness he'd carried in his soul left for good.

From there, they traveled to more far-flung places, but finally, back to the American southwest desert to settle, liking the wide open spaces. They were both ready for peace, love, and perhaps a resting place for their roving souls

They each paid cash for a new lease on life and left their pasts behind. William re-named himself William "the Dude" Makepeace. Avery bought a little white church in New Mexico, a holy structure sitting in the center of a small healing energy chakra and transformed it into Cowboy Johnson's Desert Oasis. The desert store-gas station became a sanctuary, a place where weary travelers could find rest and healing.

Mama and Geena, a runaway mother and her daughter, stopped at the desert store for gas. They discovered Avery, immediately fell in love with him, and moved in.

Despite the quiet stability Avery managed to create, the shadows of his past burdened his soul and he didn't want them known. Mama heard his name wrong when she first met him, and call him Cowboy Johnson by mistake- because he had a cowboy hat on to shade himself from the sun.

Avery accepted his new name and soon everyone was calling him Cowboy Johnson. The store became a spiritual place he hid out in against his father's hot, angry, cruel soul.

William bought the large ranch next to the desert store and became a prospector. He spent much time by himself in the desert for awhile. But he stayed close to his daughter Emma and Avery, watching as Avery poured his heart into the desert store.

When Matthew discovered the bitter truth about the drowning, he and Perry placed his wife and her two daughters in a home in France. He was drowning in guilt, but he hated the idea of facing Avery or undoing what he had done to Avery.

Matthew hated being wrong.

He finally found Avery, but he didn't go to him. Avery was running a store-gas station out in the desert and all seemed well enough there. He had plenty of time to reconcile with Avery, or so he thought. Then one day, time ended. The news of Avery's death stunned him. It was over...

But Avery's story wasn't over. And neither, it seemed, was William's...or the rest of the psychic misfits from the desert store. Time had passed, but it had been just a lull in the evil intentions awakening on the dark side.

And, the Undertaker, Crowell Goforth Restus, funeral director from another world, had an investment in the upcoming battle...

The Abduction

Avery Mott Judson woke up with his usual characteristic sense of calm. His thin body lay bony against the familiar texture of the bed beneath him.

He opened his eyes slowly, the light stinging his pupils. Another day, he thought, with the built up acceptance of years of captivity. Time had blurred in his strange captivity, and he no longer counted the days or even tried to understand the precise nature of what had happened.

He didn't know who had done it—who had stolen him from the good life he had painstakingly built at the desert store. He'd bought the little white church sitting dead center on a small, but strikingly potent vortex of energies emanating pure Goodness. He'd learned about chakra-energies in India before he discovered the little church sitting on a positive Earth chakra. He bought and converted the little church into a gas station and desert store.

He had no idea of what had become of his beloveds. His family, Mama, Geena, William, the regulars who came to the store for advice or simply to soak in the grounding energy of the place.

They were all out of reach now, and the void they left gnawed at his soul.

The day he vanished was seared into his mind. He relived it over and over again. The evil, unexpected thing flying-darting through the air had arrived in the noon day sun, blinding him, casting a shadow over the desert sand as he looked up. The thing looked like a small, red dragon with a black spade tail lashing back and forth.

Avery knew there were many unseen things that worked in the ongoing fight between Good and Evil. Avery knew this was Evil at its worst. And it was coming for him.

He froze before the immensity of the beast. It was filled with hate of anything Good. Planning to destroy the man creature below—him. It swooped down, and before Avery, who stood out back of the desert store by the fire pit, could make sense of what he was seeing, the monster pierced him through the heart and withdrew, hoping to leave a stunning amount of deadly, killing poison.

But the Goodness of the energy vortex the desert store sat in and Avery's own commitment to Goodness protected him from dying.

Stunned, Avery Mott Judson fell to the sand, his heartbeat slowed down to almost nothing from the poison. The flying creature circled to attack again. But it made the mistake of flying over the six red cactus in the little washout not far from the desert store. Six cacti made of painted red wood that Avery had built long ago to suck up anger, and all the other miseries humans carry.

The cacti, stuck in tin buckets of sand, lived off of negative energies. These days, with Avery aging and happy with Mama, the red desert cacti had shrunk and were fading, surviving off of the meager energies thrown off from the cars and trucks speeding by on the blacktopped highway nearby.

As the thing floated above them, the six wood cacti, a faded red, slumping in their tin buckets, began to swell up as they hungrily sucked the hate energy from the evil thing flying above them. Weakened, the ghastly thing wobbled in the air above them.

The red wood cacti drank in the evil greedily, happily. Soon, they were bright red and larger than they'd ever been. The evil thing floating above them had provided more than they had ever gotten from mere human beings.

When they couldn't take in any more negative energy, they let go, and the creature silently fled through the air, back to its lair where it bellowed in frustration and rage. It hadn't been able to kill the man. The man was comatose, not dead.

Vance Swain heard the creature's bellow of frustration and fear of him because it hadn't done its job. He shook his head and frowned. He couldn't trust the creature to do its job correctly. He would deal with it later. A rictus of a smile crossed his face at the thought. Then he immediately put plan B in effect.

A short time later, Vance's minions, under the guise of a hospital emergency team and ambulance, took him from Mama's arms and quickly loaded him into the ambulance and drove away, speeding through the hot desert afternoon.

Mama didn't ask any questions. She had no one there. Everybody had moved away. They two of them had lived alone at the desert store for years. She watched the ambulance drive away with her beloved inside.

The two drivers were terrified when they checked the body. Light in the body's form stayed for hours. Then other Light forms came and took much away, leaving only a dim, stubborn light glowing within the body of Avery Judson.

The ambulance fled across the desert, carrying his body. The drivers raced across the hot desert until they reached a low, sprawling, white adobe compound, and jerked to a stop. The two drivers jumped out of the ambulance and ran to their truck.

"What are you doing?" the Keeper of the compound bellowed at them.

"That's it! Never again! We're never coming back here! That's a goddamn ghost or something worse in the back of the ambulance. You deal with it!"

Their rusty old truck spun gravel as they made their escape. Sand and dust flew in the air. The Keeper of the compound stared after them.

He shouted for his men as he walked slowly over to the ambulance. Cautiously, he opened the back doors of the ambulance and looked in. He studied the waxen, white face of the comatose man lying on the gurney. The man looked harmless enough. But still, he ordered his men to put the comatose man in the first cell to the right in the long white building behind him.

"Cell number one. Maximum security. Best not to be careless. He is the Guardian of the First Gate."

The Undertaker, Crowell G. Restus, was biding his time. He knew that evil that was coming. Undertaker business in his unseen world was booming. Evil loved Death and it was growing.

In his own world, time could be bent and stretched, warped like old glass. Waiting cost him nothing. He stayed busy counteracting the contract terms of the innocents who arrived while he waited and watched over his only son, Timmon—-the Light of his own holy flame.

But Avery... Avery was different. He'd raised and protected Crowell's son Timmon. The Dark Ones wanted him. Problem was, Avery Mott Judson-alias Cowboy Johnson of the Desert Store-didn't know that his travels and spiritual learning came from a very old place in him. A place where candle light and frost lived, beckoning to him.

He didn't have the faintest clue that he was more than a survivor, more than a storekeeper. He was the Guardian of the First Gate, and evil would do everything to kill him off when the opportunity came. He would have to help him. Avery was owed that.

Chapter Two: The Waiting Game

No one questioned that Avery had a sudden heart attack and died. Ashes were swiftly returned to Mama at the store. She never knew that they were the remains of a man Vance Swain had murdered after many days filled with dark glee over the man's terror. He'd saved some of the ashes to remember that good time by. They might come in useful someday. And they had. Vance and Mina had laughed at the idea of Mama cherishing the ashes of a former devotee of Vance Swain's.

Emboldened, Mina, Vance, and their followers had attacked the Desert Store, expecting to win, but they lost the battle. Forced to flee, they fled to Colorado and nested like vipers in Mina's old haunted family mansion. A year later, Mina was slowly dying while Vance was happily planning to kill her. He wanted that thrill. Needed it. Mina knew what he was up to, escaped the mansion, and ran into the field behind it.

Mina's son Timmon, and his real father, Undertaker Crowell Goforth Restus, Master Funeral Director in another world, watched Vance Swain chase after Mina, catch her and stab her to death before stabbing himself to death. Mina was not going to be saved by the Goodness or Light waiting at the end of the field for her. They fell to the ground and died together in the too-flat field in back of Mina's family mansion, The Folly.

Crowell G. Restus, Undertaker from another world, watched every aspect of their demise carefully before he disappeared. He had to go. Timing was of the essence. Their deaths had released one who was to begin a new life. The one who hovered near death and needed his aid, had been waiting for this moment for a long time. Now was the exact moment of Avery Mott Judson's release from the hell Vance Swain and Mina had sent him to...

At the instant Vance Swain and Timmon's mother Mina died, far away, Avery Mott Judson woke up. His dream state ebbed. He was hungry. For food and news. And life. He looked around. He was in a cell of some sort. He sat up and stretched, wincing as the remnants of whatever concoction they had given him worked their way through his veins.

Pressing his hand to his chest, his heartbeat steadied, but he could still feel the phantom pain they had inflicted on him. Anger sped through him. He didn't know who *they* were, but he was certain of one thing: they had underestimated him.

To live, Avery had become a living mummy in a desert cell. He'd spent his time learning all that was around him. Time had moved slowly, and he had adapted. He learned the slow drip of water and how deep silences could be. He learned that silences were not flat lines like people in a hurry thought. Silences had their own languages. Silences were all bell curves, filled with the density of wisdom.

He had fixed his thoughts—body, mind, and soul—on the chakra the desert store rested on. He closed his eyes out of habit and focused on that connection, letting it guide him like a thread through the dark, like it had so many times before.

He imagined William sitting on the desert store porch, staring up at the stars and thinking of him. His lips curved into the faintest smile. The desert had a way of reclaiming what belonged to it.

He looked around. Silence. No one was there. His cell door stood open. Where were his jailers? Gone somewhere. He hoped they were dead.

He was going home. He knew it deep in his blood and bones. And when he got home, and when he was well again, he would search out who had done this to him, and they would pay dearly. How long had he been here? He didn't know. They kept him drugged. Time had slipped sideways, twisted like smoke. But now, time was solid again.

He would take care of Mama again. Hold her close. Make things right. Life would be good again. But not until his revenge was complete. Something evil had stolen time from him, buried him in silence, smothered him in a drugged haze, kept him locked away while time moved on without him.

He suspected Vance Swain. Vance, with his smirking, too-easy charm. Or was it his father, Matthew Judson, ruthless, powerful, and never quite free of suspicion. A man who believed appearances mattered more than truth. A man who had sent his own son away without remorse. Only rage. Maybe Matthew had sent him away again. Sorrow tugged at Avery's heart. He shrugged. It wasn't his father. It was evil magic in the form of a dragon that took him.

He stood for a long time swaying back and forth in his cell, listening to the silence that surrounded him. No more voices. Nothing. He was alone.

Hope filled him as he staggered out of the cell, gripping the wall, out into the light of day and freedom. He made his way to the center of the deserted compound, feet bare, knees buckling. The sun light stung his eyes. The sand burned his feet. Every breath he took felt borrowed. The compound was a hollow shell. Just the low hum of heat and silence.

Then he fell. So this was it. After everything, he'd die here. Alone. He lay in the hot sand and waited for his demise.

But then... a shimmer. A strange warmth filled the air, like sunlight bending wrong. And out of that shimmer stepped a man in a golden suit—pressed, gleaming, absurdly clean in the dust and ruin.

Crowell Goforth Restus.

Avery heard the name in his mind. The man radiated authority and finality. An Undertaker, going to take me from this world. An Undertaker from another world. Not from here. Not from anywhere close to here.

Well, okay. Avery thought, just before darkness took him. He blacked out. And then—cold! A splash of water to the face jerked him awake. He gasped, eyes snapping open.

The Undertaker, Crowell G. Restus, knelt beside him, silver flask in hand, an expression that might have been concern—or just polite disinterest on his golden face.

"You'll want to sit up," he said, in a voice as smooth as polished stone. "We don't have much time."

Avery wanted to laugh at his use of the word time. He blinked at the undertaker.

"So, I'm not dead?"

Crowell G. Restus gave a slight shrug.

"That depends. You were misplaced. I'm here to correct that problem. But you're not out of the woods yet, so to speak."

Avery tried to move. His arms shook. His lips were cracked. But something in him stirred with jubilation. Avery stared up at the Undertaker, vision swimming, caught between two worlds.

"William and Timmon are coming to get you." the Undertaker announced calmly, brushing dust from his golden sleeve.

"I've sent for them."

"How?"

The Undertaker gave a half-shrug, casual as if he'd just mailed a letter.

"I nudged them in my own way."

Avery blinked.

"By the way," the undertaker added, almost as an afterthought, "Timmon is my son. Thank you for adopting him as yours and raising him to the Good. That's why I'm here to help you. I owe you."

There was a quiet note of pride in his voice, like a man showing off a rare coin he'd kept hidden for years.

Avery struggled to sit up. So that's why Timmon had such power, such calm goodness—and those...odd habits.

The uncanny way Timmon always seemed to know when trouble was coming. The way he could hear things no one else could.

Avery coughed. "Did Timmon get his sense of smell from you?"

Crowell G. Restus smiled faintly, like a man indulging a joke.

"It's possible," he said. "I've always suspected he fine-tuned it himself."

Avery let out a low chuckle, which quickly turned into a grimace. Crowell offered the flask again.

"Drink. You'll need your strength. Timmon's on his way. And William... well, William's dreaming deeper than usual. Had to knock a few things off his nightstand to get his attention."

Avery was remembering.

Timmon's sense of taste and smell was so refined, he could detect things most people wouldn't believe possible. He could tell if someone had been crying three days ago by the faint salt lingering in the air around them. He could identify a lie by the sour shift in a person's body chemistry, the way fear or deceit twisted the scent just beneath their skin.

He once tasted a single spoon of stew and told the cook they'd used thyme from a shaded wall instead of full sun, and that the cow who gave the cream had been homesick. He could smell a storm coming six days out. Taste metal in the air before lightning even thought of striking. He said memory had a flavor. So did grief. So did hope.

Avery used to tease him about it. "You ought to bottle that nose and sell it to the angels." Timmon just smiled. "They already tried. I said no."

Now, Avery was starting to understand just how powerful Timmon might be, especially if Crowell G. Restus was his father. And if Timmon was coming...there was hope.

Avery drank deeply, the liquid colder than anything he'd tasted in years. He closed his eyes, his old strength beginning to seep back in. His people were coming. And when they were together again, someone or something out there was going to pay...

William and Timmon were on their way. They didn't know exactly to *where*—just that they had to go. It started with a dream, a whisper, and then a scent. Timmon had bolted upright in bed, eyes wide, nostrils flaring like a hunting dog catching the wind.

"Avery," he said simply.

He called William.

"I think Avery's still alive. Come on."

William grabbed his boots without a word. Lily raised her eyebrows.

"It's Avery."

Lily simply nodded at his hasty goodbye.

"I gotta' go. He might be still alive!"

They met at the general store. Now, they were crossing the long, hot New Mexico desert in Timmon's sun-beaten Jeep, dust trailing behind them like a ribbon of forgotten time. Timmon drove with one hand, the other hanging loosely out the window, fingers testing the heat. Every so often, he'd lift his head, sniff the air, then nod to himself.

"He's close," he muttered. "He isn't well. But not gone."

William didn't ask how Timmon knew. He just watched the horizon and waited, his pale blue eyes lit with hope and purpose. Avery might still be alive...

Avery sat up slowly, bones aching but spirit flickering with renewed light. Crowell G. Restus waited nearby, his golden suit oddly unrumpled despite the dust and sun. He checked an invisible pocket watch and sighed softly.

"I'll be going soon," he said, mostly to himself. "Things to tend to. Departures to schedule. Rest stops to arrange."

Avery looked at him. "But you'll stay long enough to see Timmon?"

Crowell smiled, his eyes glowing with a strange light. "Yes."

Avery nodded slowly, watching the golden figure fade slightly at the edges, as though his other world was beginning to reclaim him. Avery closed his eyes again. Not in pain—in peace.

Outside, somewhere in the shimmering miles of dust and sun, a Jeep tore across the desert like it had somewhere important to be. The sun was leaning westward when the Jeep finally crested a rise and stopped. Timmon shaded his eyes and squinted against the sunlight. He inhaled sharply.

"He's here," he said. "And he's still alive."

William shaded his own eyes. The compound below looked abandoned—broken fences, peeling paint, windblown silence.

"He left a scent trail," Timmon murmured. "Salt. Dust. Worn leather. But underneath it—hope. And a trace of eucalyptus, which is odd, because Avery never wore cologne.”

William said nothing, just nodded. He had his own way of knowing. His chest had started humming halfway through the drive. Not fear. Not grief. Something older. Like recognition.

Timmon started the Jeep again. They rolled to a stop just outside the compound. Timmon stepped down from the Jeep. He took two steps—then stopped. Crowell G. Restus was waiting at the threshold of the compound. His golden suit shimmered faintly in the heat.

“Hello, son,” he said, as if no time at all had ever passed. Timmon stared. His jaw clenched once, then released. He took a slow breath. And smiled.

“I thought you were just a dream,” he said. Crowell smiled faintly. “You are, too. In some places.”

William stayed back, sensing something sacred unfolding. Timmon stepped towards his father. Crowell reached out and rested his hand briefly on Timmon’s shoulder—light, steady, full of silent pride.

“You changed your name to Crowell Goforth Restus the Third,” he said.

“I had to,” Timmon replied. “It breathes better.”

Crowell’s eyes gleamed. “Good. That means you’re carrying it the right way.”

A silence passed between them, warm with things unsaid. Then Crowell stepped back.

“You’ll find him in the east wing,” he said to Timmon. “He’s waiting. Don’t take too long—he’s still fragile.”

“To the bone?” Timmon asked.

“To the soul,” Crowell replied.

And with that, Crowell G. Restus tipped his hat—a strange thing, since he hadn't been wearing one—and vanished into the heat, leaving behind a shimmer and the faint scent of marigolds and midnight.

Timmon looked at William. "Ready?"

William nodded. Together, they crossed the compound, searching for Avery.

Avery lay where the Undertaker had carried him, propped up on a dusty cot that smelled of rust and sunburned wood. He stirred in his sleep.

He was dreaming of a desert wind and the hum of a Jeep engine and he was tasting hope like an animal hopes for freedom from being trapped.

His body ached, but his spirit had begun to flicker again. Faint and wild, like the old church candlelight on winter nights when he and William used to drink tea in the back of the store and read aloud from the worn sacred books they'd picked up at roadside stalls.

And now... now he felt something in the air. Salt. Sweat. Dust. But also honey and pine and that strange metallic warmth he had always associated with William's laughter. And the wind. The wind smelled like Timmon. He heard footsteps. Boots. Two pairs. He smiled. A slow, cracked, beautiful thing. They were here.

He opened his eyes and looked at them. Was this real? Or another thing being done to him? He blinked back unexpected tears. He figured he would never see them again. But here they were.

Timmon entered first, eyes scanning every shadow. His senses flared, nose twitching slightly.

"He's in here," he whispered. "Whole."

William followed. When he saw Avery—frail, thinner, but alive—he froze. His breath caught. Avery looked up at them, voice hoarse. "Took you long enough."

William let out a laugh that cracked into a sob. "You look like hell."

"You smell like home. And you look damn old," Avery said.

"That's because I am," William answered in his high, mild voice.

Timmon crossed the room in three long strides, dropping to his knees beside the cot. He placed a hand on Avery's forehead, closed his eyes, and let out a long, measured breath.

"Still burning," he said. "Low, but steady."

William followed, knelt, and gripped Avery's hand.

"We're here now. You're not alone any more. That's over."

Avery's fingers tightened around his. "I never was. I just... forgot for a while."

They sat like that for a long time—three souls, bound by blood and history. Outside, in the fading light, a golden shimmer flickered once more at the edge of the deserted compound before vanishing entirely. Crowell Goforth Restus had seen enough. His son was with the right people now.

They sat with Avery through the night. Timmon brewed tea from herbs he carried in a leather pouch stitched with glyphs. William broke up a window to let in air and light. Avery, though weak, had color again in his face. They scrounged around and found food in the deserted kitchen in the compound and fed him.

"It was Vance Swain," Avery said, voice quiet but steady after food and water and feeling safe. "And Mina. Your mother, Timmon. They were behind this."

Timmon and William exchanged a glance. They'd both suspected, but hearing it confirmed sent a chill through the warm desert morning.

"Mina?" Timmon asked. "Why?"

"She wanted the store," Avery said. "Not just the building—the land, the chakra, the energy lines. She was tied up in something bigger. Something dark. Vance was the front man—she was the sick mind. And there was someone or someone behind *them.*"

"Someone or something bigger?" Timmon asked, frowning.

Avery nodded. "I never saw their faces. Just... glimpses. Messages. Someone rich, quiet, and protected. They didn't just want me gone. They wanted me *erased.*"

William leaned forward, voice rough. "But Vance Swain and Mina—"

"Arc dead now," Avery confirmed. "I don't know how I know. I *felt* it. That break in the dark net that held me? That must have been when they died. That's when I began to wake up."

Timmon stood and began pacing, his senses already searching the air for more.

"Those two were gatekeepers," he muttered. "Pawns in someone else's hands."

William stated grimly, "Then there are others who still out there."

Avery met his eyes. "Yes. There are. And I'm not hidden anymore. But you'll have to protect me until I'm well again."

Timmon stopped pacing. "Then we dig. Quietly. Carefully. And when we're sure—we strike. But first, we get you well again."

Outside, the wind began to shift, rolling across the compound with a new voice—older, colder. There were names still unspoken. Power still hidden. And justice, long overdue...

The three of them—Avery, Timmon, and William the Dude—were together again. The Dark Ones were enraged. Vance and Mina were dead. Two of their minions lost. And, Avery Mott Judson had escaped the compound when the cowards fled. He was alive. He could foil their plans. They would attack him. Take him out. Kill him and the Goodness living in him. But to do it, they would have to take out the vortex of energy he was Guardian of, the oldest, the most essential of five energy vortexes of Light. They began to plan...

Chapter Three: Return to the Desert Store

By late afternoon, the Jeep reached the desert store. The desert had worn it down some, but the energy pulsing beneath the store was still alive. Timmon felt it in his bones. William felt it in the quiet joy settling in his heart. Avery? He felt it in his soul. He stepped over the threshold and paused, eyes closed.

"Still humming," he whispered. "After all this time."

The Desert Store was more than a gas station–grocery store. More than the little white church it once was. The desert store sat dead center in a rare convergence of positive, healing energy—a Good healing chakra that extended like invisible roots for miles.

People were drawn to it without knowing why or questioning it. They came not just for gas, groceries, handmade goods, the desert honey, or the quiet peace... they came because the place itself *healed* them. Which was exactly why someone or something wanted it destroyed.

Avery limped slowly past the old counter, brushing dust from the shelves, the wood, the hanging signs. Then he stopped. There was a low creaking sound—familiar, but slightly off.

Timmon was already moving. "There's something back here," he said, nose twitching. "Ink. Wax. Old steel. And..." he paused, eyes narrowing, "lavender and iron filings. That's warding magic. Hidden magic."

William followed them toward the back wall until all three stood beneath the portrait of the church's original founders. Avery hesitated. He'd studied that painting a thousand times. But he had never touched it. Now he reached forward, lifted the frame... and it *clicked.* A panel in the wall slid open with a soft, tired sigh. Inside was a narrow wood drawer, almost invisible unless you knew where to feel. Avery slid it out carefully.

There was a folded map inside—hand-drawn on linen parchment—along with a small copper disk etched with old runes and a lock of hair wrapped in silk thread. Timmon took one look and paled.

"This wasn't just a desert store," he said. "This was a *barrier.* A guardian point."

William frowned. "Against what?"

Timmon looked up, his eyes troubled. "Against something very old. Something that feeds on good energy. Someone—or something—was trying to weaken this place. If it had fallen completely... the whole region would've cracked open to the other side."

Avery gripped the map. "That's why they came after me. I'm guessing I was the Keeper. The anchor."

"And someone wanted the anchor gone," Timmon said grimly.

William exhaled. "So... who wished it gone?"

Avery's jaw clenched. "Someone who wanted power but couldn't get past the Light without first dimming it."

Timmon traced a sigil on the copper disk and hissed.

"These are priest marks. But not the good kind. These were meant to *hollow out* holy places. This wasn't just personal."

"No," Avery said. "It was a first move in a bigger war."

Now they had proof. And a reason to fight back. Timmon unfolded the map on the old store counter, brushing off the dust with reverence. Strange lines curled across the parchment—some familiar trails, others clearly veiled symbols of energy flows, ley lines, and places of power. At the very center was the desert store, marked with a shining sunburst. But over it, in faded red ink, was a scrawl: **"Claimed by SSD. As of Emma's Departure. Store Closed. Energy contained. Fence constructed."**

Avery's hand trembled. "Susan Sugar Diamond," he muttered.

William's head snapped up. "The Queen of novelists who writes all those famous orphan books?"

"That's her," Avery said. "She moved the orphanage out to the ranch after Emma left for Europe. Said it was better for the children—more space, more sun. Claimed the old church-store property under her name. Fenced it off. Sealed it."

"But *why* close the store?" William asked. "She could've left it open. The energy helped people. You helped people."

Timmon answered. "Because of the children, I guess. She didn't want them dealing with what she discovered here."

Timmon said, his voice low. "If the store is a guardian point—and it is—then closing it and moving the orphanage from here out to the ranch was a damn smart move."

William frowned. "Then who's behind all this?"

The light inside the old store flickered. The sun suddenly broke through a window and beamed directly on the copper disk. The disc began to hum.

Avery couldn't take any more. Of anything. He was still weak and tired. He turned away and wandered out front. He sat down on the stoop of the old church store, the cracked wood warm beneath him, the desert wind whispering across his face like it was trying to soften what couldn't be softened.

They had told him on the drive to the store— quietly, gently—just after the sun had gone down and the stars began blinking through the heat haze, that his beloved Mama was gone. Peacefully. Beautifully. In Spain. With his son by her side.

The grief hit him sideways. He felt it now like a fault line beneath his ribs. Mama was gone. And the three Wise Men? Bud Spinner, Ben, and Andy, from Mama's home town? Still living in the monastery in Oregon, tucked into their routines of silence and strange, sacred knowledge. They had survived. William said they lit candles for Avery every Friday, never missing a week. Never saying in any way that he was dead.

And Emma...his beloved daughter with her secret room filled with a huge library of romance novels. Emma had at last married. She'd married a man named Alexander and moved to Spain. She'd given up the ranch to Susan Sugar Diamond to use as an orphanage. Alexander was supposed to be a prince of a man, by all accounts. The kind who spoke little but listened deeply, who moved through the world like he belonged in both the garden and the stars. And he loved Emma.

Too much time had passed. Avery let the ache wash through him. He didn't try to stop it. There was a lot of lost time he needed to grieve. Too many yesterdays that had slipped from his hands while he lay in that hollow, stolen place. He closed his eyes.

Timmon and William were inside, sorting out the mystery of the copper disk and map. The store was waking up again—he could feel it. But this moment was his. Just him and the ghosts of what once was.

A small desert bird hopped near his foot. He opened his eyes and nodded at it. "She would've liked you," he murmured. "Mama always said birds carry messages. Maybe you'll fly one back to her."

The bird tilted its head, then fluttered off into the dusk. A long time later, Avery took a deep breath and stood. Much had changed. Years had been stolen. But he was back. And there were still things left to do.

The three men sat around the long table in the back of the store as the sun melted into the horizon, casting long, gold shadows through the open back door. The copper disk hummed gently between them, forgotten for now. There were heavier truths to carry. Timmon did the talking. He had the voice for it— quiet, steady, like a man delivering weather reports from the edge of the world. Avery listened, jaw clenched, heart opening and breaking with every word.

"Geena's not well," Timmon said. "After you were taken, she waited for a while. But then the hope drained out of her. She went back to Ray. Teaches a bit. Drinks too much. Doesn't talk much. But we think... she's waiting still."

Avery bowed his head.

"Celia's another story," Timmon went on. "Took her pain and turned it into fire. Went to the mountains. Joined a warrior circle. Women who train with blades and read runes in the rain. They say she can catch an arrow mid-flight now. I wouldn't doubt it."

Avery managed a soft, hoarse chuckle. "That sounds like her."

"Normaine and Eddy are still upstate," Timmon said. "Got a little farm near a river. Normaine hammers out art for a gallery in New York City. Eddy builds boats now. Quiet life, but good."

Avery blinked. "I thought they hated water."

Timmon shrugged. "Turns out they just hated crowds." There was a silence then. A deeper one. Timmon's voice dropped. "The Mafia Sisters are gone."

Avery didn't move.

"Like leaves in the wind," Timmon said softly. "Each one in her own way. No trace. No goodbyes."

William never said a word through all of it. He sat tight beside Avery, one shoulder pressed against his, a steady presence. No explaining. No pity. Just *there*. Finally, as the dusk curled in around them, William shifted slightly, looked out the window, then grinned.

"I'm still with Lily Jean Bloome," he said.

Avery turned toward him.

William gave a lazy shrug. "She figured I'd wander off. I didn't. She says I've matured. I say I just got slower."

Avery smiled. For the first time in years, he smiled deep.

The world had cracked and bent, but here they were. Timmon. William. Him. Still breathing. Still burning.

"We don't need to go out to the ranch," Timmon said, folding the map carefully and slipping it back into his satchel. "It's an orphanage now. Well-staffed. Well-run. Boys' and girls' quarters. Clean food. Honest caretakers. Susan Sugar Diamond has done a good job with it."

Avery exhaled slowly, relief flickering in his chest like the first cool breeze after a sandstorm.

"So, the kids are safe," he said.

Timmon nodded. "Safer than they've been in a long time. The current director's a retired nun who walks with a cane and swears like a sailor. You'd like her."

William chuckled. "Does she serve peach pie on Sundays?"

Timmon gave a rare grin. "Only to the well-behaved and the especially unruly."

Avery leaned back in his chair, the tension beginning to bleed from his shoulders.

"Good," he said. "Then we can focus on what matters now. Whoever signed Susan's name— whoever hid behind her to weaken this place—*they're still out there.*"

He looked toward the altar at the far end of the store, where the light from the copper disk glinted like a tiny sunrise.

"This place was meant to protect," he said. "We can't let them turn it into something else."

Timmon was already unrolling a second parchment from his satchel—one he hadn't shown them yet.

"Then it's time you saw this," he said.

Avery and William leaned in. The parchment showed a larger map—an intricate web of light points, lay lines, and hidden locations. The desert store was one of the light points.

"This isn't the only guardian post," Timmon said, his voice low. "There are more. And someone's been trying to corrupt them."

Avery looked up, eyes sharpening. "Then we will rebuild this one."

William cracked his knuckles. "And find the rest."

Timmon tapped a glowing point on the far edge of the map. "The one in the west just went dark."

They stared at the point in silence.

The fight wasn't over.

It was just beginning.

Avery stared at the glowing map, his brow furrowed. The lines pulsed with quiet light, the smaller guardian points marked like tiny suns scattered across forgotten corners of the land. "This is... familiar," he said softly. "But I don't know why."

Timmon watched him closely. "Because your soul remembers."

Avery's eyes flicked toward him, startled. Timmon nodded, calm and sure. "You were part of this. Not as Avery Judson, son of Matthew. But before. Before names and blood and the weight of that accusation. Before the desert store."

Avery looked down at his hands, tracing the old calluses from working on cars, the small scar on his palm from a childhood fall. "I've felt it sometimes. Like I've been here before. Not just *here,* but *this.*"

William spoke gently, "You always had a way with the store. Like it breathed through you."

Timmon unrolled the older part of the map—a parchment cracked with age, filled with strange symbols and half-faded glyphs. In the center, the desert store was marked not with a sun—but a figure. A man with one hand open, and light pouring from it. Avery leaned closer, breath catching.

"That symbol," he whispered. "I've drawn that in the margins of notebooks. I used to sketch it without knowing why."

"Because your soul has always known," Timmon said. "This wasn't just your refuge. You are one of the Anchors. The ones chosen to hold the balance of a Guardian point. You have a soul bond with this land."

Avery leaned back, the weight of knowing pressing against his chest.

"Why didn't I remember?"

"Because you weren't supposed to," Timmon said quietly. "Not until the danger returned. Not until your being was strong enough to carry it again."

William placed a steady hand on Avery's shoulder. "You're strong enough now."

Avery looked toward the altar again. The light from the copper disk flickered like it heard everything.

"I don't know what I'm supposed to do."

"You don't need to," Timmon said. "Your soul knows."

And in that moment, Avery felt it—a faint stirring beneath his ribs. Like roots stretching, old roots, deeper than any name. The map glowed again, and somewhere far away, another guardian point flickered... as if waiting for him to remember the rest. But it wasn't time. Not yet.

Timmon studied the short, stubborn, green-eyed man with unexpected tenderness. It would take the battle itself to wake Avery up to who he was. And Timmon knew why Avery kept on not knowing: because knowing changed a man. Changed the way he loved. Avery would never love Mama in the same way again once he knew the truth.

Timmon shook his head. That was why he and Celia so often clashed. She was warrior—big, strong, beautiful, brimming with energy. Her philosophies were grounded in the physical and the emotional, all fire and force.

His path was different: rooted in the scent and sense of things, the subtle currents others overlooked. He was more refined than she would ever be. He sighed.

Chapter Four: The Work Begins

Avery stayed behind in New Mexico with William while Timmon went north to his land. The desert store near Albuquerque was Avery's heart, his charge, his soul's unfinished work. The land still pulsed with quiet energy—a big open space, warm, steady, and waiting. He worked alongside William, rebuilding the store by hand—beam by beam, stone by stone—restoring it not to what it once was, but to what it was meant to become.

They read the land like a scripture. Every window angle, every grain of wood mattered. The altar faced north-northwest, just as Timmon had instructed him. And beneath it, the copper disk continued to hum.

Avery and William built alone—until those meant to help began arriving on their own. Travelers. Seekers. Children of the light who didn't know why they came, only that they were drawn to the desert store. Some swept floors. Some left stones at the doorway. Some said nothing at all, only stayed the night and wept beside the humming copper altar.

William stayed close. Quiet, steady. Fixing hinges. Holding silence when it was needed. Smiling only for Avery. The two men did not speak of the years lost. Only of the Light returning...

Colorado had called Timmon home like black thunder in deep rock. He returned to his property in the high land outside Gitwell—pine-shadowed, wind-sung, wild and mountain high to the sky. *Crazy Jack, Lou, and Gordon were working with him.* They were building the Colorado Light Point. Crazy Jack, with his surprising oratory sensitivity to crowds. Lou, who gardened and cooked like she was carving prayers. Who cooked like Jesus was coming to supper. Gordon, who read people's faces like they were fault lines in fate.

Timmon's land in Colorado was strange, but not in the dramatic, mountain-hewn way folks expected of Colorado. His stretch of land lay flat and wind-swept, high on a plain where the horizon stretched so wide it made your heart ache. The wind never quite stopped. It carried the scent of pine from the western edge of the property and whispers from something far older beneath the soil. Buried in the dust and grass were flecks of gemstone—pink quartz, turquoise, sunstone, tiny red garnets, and something else harder to name. They weren't scattered randomly, either. All of the stones *marked something.* Lou said it felt like the veins of an old celestial creature that had once slept beneath the Earth.

Part of the property dipped into pine-shadowed ridges, dark green against the winter's cold. That's where the circle stones nestled. Weathered, half-sunken, older than any recorded map. Timmon knew—*that's where the guardian's heart lay.*

Timmon led them to the ridge on his property where the guardian point slumbered, half-lost under old stone and snow-bleached soil. They began there.

Crazy Jack had already claimed the nearby village as his own. Gitwell, Colorado. Once a dusty place with a bad reputation—haunted by the sick, the twisted, and the ghost-bitten. Its name had been ironic for decades. Folks came to Gitwell and usually didn't get better.

But things had shifted. After a few months of Crazy Jack's hollering, sign-painting, well-digging, chicken-adopting, and flat-out stubborn refusal to let the town die, they made him mayor. By accident. No one ran against him.

Mayor "Crazy Jack" now ran weekly 'spirit reconciliation meetings' in the old saloon, cleaned up the graveyard, and chased out the worst of the bad winds with a smudge stick and a trumpet.

Mina's ancestral home—*Manfred's Folly*—still stood. Once a place of heavy curtains, black mirrors, and curses buried under floorboards, it had rebuilt itself into a quiet, morose, square little cottage. Sage grew in thick circles around it. Lou planted the sage with her own hands, whispering prayers in three languages—old, new, and in between. Gordon said the Folly no longer *bit*. Now, it watched and waited...

Timmon stood at the edge of the circle of stones, the Colorado wind tugging at his coat. He'd begun mapping the energy lines, aligning the stones, and speaking to the land in ways his father, Crowell Goforth Restus the Second, had once done. This Guardian Point was colder, older, slower to trust, but it was waking up...

Back in New Mexico, Avery and William continued rebuilding the store. By day, the work moved steadily—sun-worn lumber fitted into new frames, walls raised like prayers, the copper disk set beneath the altar now pulsing with steady warmth. Travelers came and went. Stories were told.

But by night, Avery dreamed. Dark dreams of shadowed rooms and silent screams. Of voices twisted to mimic love. Of a childhood stripped and rewritten by other people's sins. He woke up sweating, fists clenched, heart pounding. William never asked. He just sat close. Kept the coffee hot. Kept the silence kind.

But Avery stayed *angry*. Not at William. Not at Susan Sugar Diamond or Mina. He was angry at how much time had been stolen from him. How long he'd been trapped. How *easily* people had believed he was dead, then moved on.

One morning, before the sun had fully risen, he packed a back pack with water, a flask, two pistols, and ammunition.

"I'm going out," he said.

William simply nodded. "The red cactus desert? It's about time."

Avery didn't answer, but that was answer enough. He drove out to the red sand—an isolated stretch of forgotten desert where, once, long ago, he had placed the six red-painted wooden cacti in buckets over the ridge and away from the store. He had built it as a place to release anger back then. It had been his—Avery-Cowboy Johnson's place for release. A ritual site for anger, sorrow, grief too large to carry inside. A place to shoot, shout, cry, to release anger. But he was no longer willing to be Cowboy Johnson because Mama was gone. Dead.

Now, he would be just Avery Mott Judson, son of Matthew Mark Judson, brother of Perry, for he was a man resurrected from the dead.

Avery stood before the half-buried stubs of the old red cactus guardians, the sun harsh and high above, hot wind tugging at him. He drew his pistol—not to make sense of anything, but because *nothing* else had worked.

He fired into the sand, into the sky, into the silence—then finally, into the wooden stubs themselves. The first bullet hit the nearest cactus square on. A dull thud. Then something... shifted. A hum. A shimmer. The air thickened for just a breath—like old memories rising from deep inside the ground. The next bullet struck another stub—and a *crack* rang out, not from wood splitting, but from *something waking*. The final shots—angry, ragged, *pure*—were fired directly into what was left of the six. And the desert caught fire. Not flame, but *color*.

The wood stubs pulsed red—bright, blinding red, as if the paint hadn't faded but simply *rested*. Sand whipped up and peeled away. The buckets the six red cacti stood in rattled.

The cacti, once tired and sinking, stood tall again, shaking off dust, soaking in Avery's fury like water. They *loved* negative energy. That was their gift. Their design. What he'd made them for. Anger. Grief. Pain. Rage. They drank it all in—every scream and shout, every shot, every shattered thought. And in return, they stood stronger. Red. Bright. Radiant.

Avery fell back into the sand, panting. Laughing. Crying. It wasn't destruction. It was *feeding.* The red cactus he had built weren't for shame or repression. They were built to hold what no man should have to carry alone.

Slowly, the wind died down. The desert stilled. The cacti gleamed like he'd painted them just that morning.

Avery felt lighter. Not healed—not yet. But *carried.* And that was enough. He whispered, "Thank you," then turned toward the desert store in the distance—the tip of its steeple, just visible, waiting like a friend who knew the worst parts of a person and stayed anyway.

The sun had just begun to dip behind the hills when Avery returned to the desert store. His coat was streaked with dust, the brim of his cap pulled low. His shoes were scuffed, and the smell of gunpowder clung faintly to his clothes like a memory.

William was sitting on the steps of the store, sipping coffee from a chipped mug, watching the sky turn honey-colored. He didn't say anything at first. Just looked up and took Avery in, head to toe.

William had been mulling over the changes in Avery. Avery was always a stubby, stocky kid—chubby-faced, broad-shouldered, with a softness that clung to him through youth and well into middle age. No matter what life threw at him, Avery had never lost those boyish curves, that built-in comfort. But now...

Now, he was lean and clean, almost holy in a peculiar way. Had he meditated all this time? Like they both learned in India?

The long years of absence—and whatever had happened in that time—had stripped him down to sinew and sharpness. His body had narrowed, angles showing where roundness used to be. His brown hair was gone, replaced by stark white hair, worn in a braid down his back. Just like William's.

The changes were striking. Almost jarring. His softness, the physical warmth of him, had faded. William hoped he still had some of it left—somewhere beneath the taut lines and weathered skin. His old sweetness. His quiet, steady kindness that made people stay, made them feel safe. He didn't say any of what he was thinking out loud. But he watched. And he remembered.

Avery walked slowly, shoulders straighter than when he'd left the compound, jaw set, but softer around his green eyes. He stopped at the foot of the steps and looked up. "They're back."

William blinked. "The cacti?"

Avery nodded. "They took it. Every last bit of it. Rage, grief, all of it. Drank it up like old friends. They're standing tall again—paint glowing like it was never gone."

William stood and stepped down to meet him. He studied Avery's face, the way the lines had changed. Not fewer—but truer.

"I figured," William said quietly. "I felt it. Something in the wind shifted. Like the land exhaled."

Avery smiled a steady smile. "I think they forgave me."

"For what?" William asked. Avery looked off toward the horizon. "For waiting too long to come home."

William reached into his pocket, pulled out a rag, handed it to Avery. "You got red paint on your shirt. Or blood. Hard to tell with you sometimes."

Avery laughed. Full and real. They stood there awhile in the twilight, just the two of them, dusted in desert light. No more questions. No need for them. Finally, William nudged him with an elbow. "Come on in the store, Avery. No need to stay out here now. It's over. You did good. I made stew. The good kind. I even chopped the onions instead of weeping over them."

"Miracle," Avery said, climbing the steps beside him. "Guess we're all rebuilding something."

William grinned. "Yeah. But not from scratch. From memory."

Inside, the copper disk beneath the altar pulsed once. As if in agreement.

Night had settled deep, stars sharp above the desert store, when the wind shifted again—not in temperature, but in *tone*. A tone that said, pay attention- someone's coming.

They were eating. William looked up from his bowl of stew first. He tilted his head, nostrils flaring slightly, spoon in the air. Then he smiled in that quiet, knowing way he always did when the world surprised him just right. He laid his spoon down. Avery, halfway through eating, noticed the stillness and laid his spoon down, too. Warm, sweet air filled the store's back room where they sat.

Not silence—just that sweet anticipation. The kind that came before something sacred enters a room. Sure enough, a soft knock sounded on the door. Three knocks. Three times. Rhythmic. Certain.

William didn't bother to ask who it might be. He went to the door and opened it. There she stood. Lily Jean Bloome. His love, his life. Long dark coat, desert boots dusted red. Her lovely white hair gathered in a braid that shimmered silver under the moonlight. Her smoky eyes—those steady, watchful, story-filled eyes—met William's like they'd never looked away.

"Hello, my dear," she said, her voice like quiet thunder. "I'm hoping I brought the rest of the story."

William stepped back and let her in, his smile blooming like it always did just for her. "Took your sweet time."

Lily Jean Bloome studied Avery. "You're the man the land won't shut up about."

She smiled.

"I didn't know…"

"That I'm a Guardian Keeper?" she finished for him, gently. "William is not one to brag. But it's true. I carry the lineage. I've held knowledge until it was time to speak it. And now—*it's time.*"

She walked to the altar, placed one hand on the copper disk. It pulsed under her palm like a heart recognizing kin.

"The red cacti flared and rose, Avery. You did a good job. Every Keeper still attuned felt it. It gave them all warm, red courage. Every Guardian Point still intact is *watching.* The network is waking. Trouble is, that means something else is waking too."

William stirred the stew without looking away.

"What others?"

"Some of the gatekeepers are still alive. Some lost. A few... corrupted."

She looked at Avery. "That's why your place in this desert store matters so much. It's not just a post. It's the *heartline.* The oldest pulse. If it falls again, the rest will unravel."

Avery took her words in slowly, the weight of truth finally given shape. Lily Jean Bloome took off her coat, hung it on a nail, and rolled up her sleeves. "But we're not going to let that happen. Not this time."

William handed her a bowl of stew and smirked at Avery.

"Told you she was the smart one."

Avery smiled back, quiet fire in his eyes. The Keeper of Guardians was here now.

Later, the fire crackled low in the stone hearth. The night air was cool. Shadows danced along the beams of the desert store. Lily Jean Bloome sat cross-legged on an old rug by the altar, the copper disk resting in her lap. Avery sat across from her, alert and quiet. William leaned against the open back doorway, arms crossed, watching the stars with one ear tuned to their every word.

She touched the edge of the disk. "You've been focused on Vance and Mina," she said softly. "They played the part of the villain to draw your fire. But they were pawns. Nothing more."

Avery stiffened. "Pawns of *what?*"

She set the disk aside and leaned forward.

"Something older than our bloodlines. Something that doesn't want to own the Earth—it wants to *undo* it. The Guardian Points? They're not just sacred spots. They're locks. Ancient seals. They keep the nasty sleeping things *asleep*."

William moved closer. "You're saying something's trying to break the locks?"

She nodded. "And not by brute force. By erosion. By unraveling one point at a time until the entire lattice collapses. Vance and Mina didn't know the full scale. They were seduced by promises—power, influence, immunity. They were used to *soften the land*. Mina was especially useful—she knew the energy, even if she twisted it."

Avery's voice was low. "So what happens if the whole web goes down?"

Her gaze didn't waver. "The Veil lifts. The barriers between the living world and the void beneath thin so much that the old, evil hungers can come through. Not all at once—first in whispers, then in plagues. Places like this become haunted in ways you can't cleanse."

She stood and placed her hand on the altar. The disk beneath it pulsed like a warning.

"This point—the desert store—is the tuning fork. The first drumbeat. The oldest pulse. It was the first site chosen when the lattice was spun."

William's voice was quiet. "And someone wants to kill it."

"Yes," she said. "So we have to rebuild it not just as it was—but stronger. And we have to be ready."

Avery's eyes narrowed. "Ready for evil to attack, right?"

She glanced at the dark desert outside the window.

"Yes. For the ones who trained and used Vance and Mina and then destroyed them. The ones who never show their faces. The ones who *remember the Guardians wars from before.*"

Chapter Five: Building

The air in the room cooled as though the night itself leaned in to listen. Moments passed like wind unseen, moving across the highway out front and through the folds of the desert.

William watched Avery taking the information in. He sighed with love. Avery was as much an innocent in his own way as Mama had ever been!

"They are not done with you." William said softly. Now you know why they want to destroy you."

"Yes."

"Without this place and you standing strong against the evil, the rest of the guardians haven't got a chance."

"Yes."

William and Lily Jean Bloome watched as Avery changed. Confusion and sorrow left his face and it lit with determination.

"Good." Lily Jean Bloome said. "
Now let's get our buts in gear and go forward. We got a lot to do before all hell breaks loose."...

The evil kept growing. Not like a fire leaping from tree to tree, but like roots burrowing deep, spreading in silence until the ground itself was theirs. The Dark Ones had felt the stir in Avery's chest, the faint pulse of his soul remembering, and it made them angry. They focused all their strength on what mattered most: Killing Avery Mott Judson, the Guardian of the First Gate. And they would not simply come for him. They would overcome every Point of Light this time.

And at the attacks center stood Avery—unaware that when the first blow fell, it might fall hardest on him.

Avery worked with his hands every day. They strengthened once again and became rough, calloused, cracked from sun and effort. William worked beside him, steady, unshakable. Lily Jean Bloome mapped energy lines in the early mornings and made sharp, comforting tea at night.

Others began showing up. Old customers, a lost mechanic from Gallup, a woman who'd once slept on the floor of the store twenty years ago and never forgot the peace it gave her. Then more. Volunteers. Builders. Dreamers. Folks who didn't know *why* they came, only that they *had* to. Some stayed for a day. Some stayed for good. Tents and trailers. The gas pumps went in—restored, bright green and white, glowing each night under the moon.

They rebuilt the garage. Not just a service bay—*a repair station for the road-worn and soul- heavy.* Old cars, broken belts, lost travelers. All welcome.

The desert store breathed with good vibes again...

Hundreds of miles to the north, Timmon and his crew were shaping something very different—but equally sacred. In Colorado, the wind stayed cold. The Colorado soil remembered earlier wars. But Timmon's land was waking.

Crazy Jack had cleared out Gitwell's Main Street. The saloon was now a hall of books and resting benches and weather storm warning exchanges. Pine and cedar benches lined Main street.

Outside of town on Timmon's land, under the gemstones his land began a strong pulse, the winds singing their songs over the gemstones. The elder circle of stones had realigned themselves and stood near the pine edges of the property, taller now—marked, blessed.

The Guardian points were beginning to hold. Two anchor sites now strengthened. Two hearts beating across state lines. And somewhere out there, S*omething* felt it. Something stirred, restless and aware. The light was coming back. And so, in turn, the larger Shadow began to stretch...

The work on the desert store was finished. Cowboy Johnson's Desert Oasis stood proud again—not just rebuilt, but stronger than ever before. Windows gleamed. The roof shimmered faintly under night stars. The copper disk beneath the altar hummed in rhythm with the wind. Gas pumps clicked smoothly, the garage smelled of clean oil and desert sage, and the store shelves—lined with hand-labeled goods, maps, charms, and preserves—seemed to glow from within.

Everything was polished. Everything ran smoothly. Even time seemed to move more smoothly and efficiently now. And above it all—the *Light*. No longer just a subtle pulse. The Light had become a *Beam*. Clear, strong, pointing *north*.

Working in unison, the misfits began to understand why they had once lived at the desert store, and why the new people had been drawn in.

They knew now that they were all part of a larger purpose. None of their life had been an accident, not from the first moment.

Life had brought them back together in this place to serve a higher purpose. Their souls lifted, their kinks and oddments were sensible-and practical- to all of their delight! They laughed and loved again, and plied their "gifts" openly until the work was finished...

At last the Guardian Point on Timmon's land in Colorado stood anchored and whole. Crazy Jack kept busy issuing psychic weather forecasts, while Lou quietly carved runes into windowsills with a smile because her own true heart love, Gordon, worked beside her.

At last, when all was ready, the two points of Light joined each other across the miles, two ancient drums beating in tandem again for the first time in ages. Everyone celebrated. They knew that the balance was shifting in their favor. The Veil was thinning. Sooner or later, the evil ones would challenge them. But they would be as ready as they could be...

It was just past dusk when a visitor arrived. He rode in a battered truck that smelled like ash and electricity. He stepped out of his truck. His boots were scorched at the soles. His coat carried red dust from a place no one at the desert store had ever seen. Avery watched him, one hand instinctively resting on the doorframe. William stood behind Avery, silent but alert. Lily Jean Bloome stood guard at the altar, the copper disk flickering pale violet.

The man looked at them with eyes dark as storm glass. And *tired.* He didn't speak right away. He took off his hat, pressed it to his chest.

Then, quietly: "They're testing the northern gate. Timmon's holding... for now."

The air dropped a degree. William's jaw tightened. Avery felt his spine go cold. Lily Jean Bloome stepped forward.

"What name do you carry?"

The man hesitated, then said: "Lady, you may call me Hollis. I walked through the third Point of Light. What's left of it."

Avery's voice, low and steady: *"What's left?"*

The man named Hollis nodded grimly. "The Third gate fell two days ago. Burned from the inside. No one survived. Just the Sequoias. It... *opened* something. Something hungry."

He looked at each of them in turn.

"I came here because this place still *shines.* I came here... to warn you."

Silence fell like ash. The wind picked up, brushing the porch bells, carrying the scent of sage and metal. Timmon sniffed the air. Not yet, but it was coming.

Late that night, after the fire faded down into crackling embers, the man named Hollis, quiet, hollow-eyed, road-worn, slept in his bedroll by the fire. They made space for him without question, offered him a motel room. He shook his head.

"I'll sleep out here by the fire if you don't mind."

He nodded at the fire, set down his pack, and accepted a tin cup of coffee like it was the first kind thing he'd held in months. The desert store protected those who belonged, and it knew Hollis needed shelter before he could carry on. He slept long the first night.

The second night, he walked the perimeter of the energy chakra the buildings stood in, eyes tracking the sky, sensing things others couldn't name. The third night, he helped hang a mobile made of copper bells and old silver spoons.

"Sound's gotta move jist' right," he murmured. By the fourth day, he was different. Stronger. Steadier. Eating. Resting. But still not whole. At dawn, he gathered his things together.

"Where are you headed now?" William asked, not expecting an answer.

Hollis shrugged. "North. Somethin's pulling me that way."

Lily nodded. "Timmon's place. Guardian ground."

Hollis looked back once at the store, hand brushing the doorframe like a farewell to something sacred.

"Tell your daughter Emma I Thankee. Her painting scared off the thing that followed me."

Then he was gone.

"Don't know what he is talking about. Emma is in Europe," William said, shaking his head, annoyed. "I don't want little Emma in this war."

"Who knows what strange things are going on these days?" Lily Jean Bloome said calmly.

She went and stood before the map unrolled on the store's altar, her hand hovering over the East.

"We've rebuilt the South and the North. The West flickers, but is not yet gone. The East has not awakened."

"And the Center?" Avery asked.

She looked at him for a long time. "The Center will reveal itself only when the others are aligned."

William stepped closer. "And if they never align?"

Her voice lowered as if someone might be listening. Her voice was barely above a whisper.

"Then the lattice collapses. And something *gets in* to this world that doesn't know the meaning of mercy."

They stared at each other—three old people with silver hair braided down their backs. All three taller than they should be, thinner than they had any business being. Where were their rocking chairs? Their disability checks? Their slow mornings and afternoon naps?

Instead, they had an unfinished map, a flickering beam of Light, and a desert store sitting atop a pulse of pure ancient Goodness. They had stumbled into an adventure that might take their lives sooner than expected—not that they had so much left—no cozy retirement homes, no bingo halls, no final chapters wrapped in routine. Just magic-and joining the ongoing fight so Goodness would prevail over Evil.

A hush settled between them. The kind of silence that settles in when people know what's at stake and choose to stand anyway.

William snorted softly. "Well, guess this means I can stop filling out all that Medicare paperwork."

Avery cracked a grin. "And I was *this close* to ordering a leather recliner with a built-in snack tray."

Lily Jean Bloome raised an eyebrow. "You two are free to retire anytime. But not until this war is over. Then you two can lay around as much as you like."

They all laughed—quiet, dry, a little cracked at the edges. But real. They weren't young. They weren't ready. They needed naps. But they were *here*. And for now, that was enough.

That night, out behind the desert store, they lit a fire beneath the stars. The air was cool and dry, the flames crackling softly in the pit William had lined with old river stones. The scent of sand and sage drifted upward into the dark sky above them. The stars blinked slowly, like they were listening.

The three of them sat on old crates and folding chairs. Avery, William, and Lily Jean Bloome, boots dusty, bellies warm with fresh rabbit stew. They passed around an old canteen and shared stories in the slow way people do when they've earned their stories the hard way.

Chapter Six: Pick Up Sticks

Far to the west, beyond the mountains and deep in a forest of giant Sequoias in northern California, two travelers were driving an old blue van towards a Light beam. The beam was weak and went out intermittently. Still, it was strong enough for Hattie and Beck to keep following.

Hattie was small and fast-talking, cute and pert. She was gabby and naïve, childish, rarely thinking things through. But that was before. Now, she was maturing, with Beck by her side. Hattie was a House Whisperer. Her baby blues could spot a crooked curtain from fifty feet outside a house. She had a talent for listening to the bones of a house and talking to them. She could walk into an abandoned house, press her palm to a wall, and feel what had happened there—who'd loved, who'd lied, who'd died, and who'd never quite left, dead or alive.

Beck, her partner, was a Tree Whisperer. Beck was medium height, quiet and dark haired and gentle mannered, except when trees talked back to him. Beck could lean against the bark of an old cedar and learn more than most folks could from an entire book.

Hattie and Beck. Almost opposites in personalities, the two of them were in love—quietly, steadily, without needing to name it too often. They camped in their old blue van with a kettle that always smelled faintly of cinnamon and road dust. They traveled west, towards the flickering beam of Light they'd both seen in their dreams.

They didn't know yet that they were part of something much larger. But the Earth did. And soon, so would they.

They hoped the towering, ancient Sequoias might tell them about the curious Light steadily drawing them to the west coast. Beck suspected the ancient trees knew things buried too deep for maps.

The rusty old van hummed down a narrow two-lane road that wound down through foothills smelling of dust, wild fennel, and old secrets. Hattie leaned out the window, singing to herself—a half lullaby, half blues tune about a chicken who escaped a wedding. Beck drove with one hand on the wheel, the other resting lightly in his lap, his eyes scanning the horizon the way some people read omens in clouds.

They didn't speak for a while. Nothing was wrong. The road was speaking louder than either of them. Suddenly, Beck slowed. Ahead, near a bend where the road dipped between two sycamore trees, a figure stood beside a rusted-out sign. Not hitchhiking. Not waving. Just standing.

Hattie sat up. "Do you see...?"

"I do," Beck said, his voice low, careful.

The figure was dressed in a long coat, colorless, dust-covered. A wide hat shaded their face. In their hand, they held what looked like an old walking stick carved with symbols that shimmered faintly.

Beck rolled the van to a slow stop.

Hattie locked her door and rolled down the window a couple inches. "Can we help you?"

The figure didn't move at first. Then the stranger lifted his head, just enough to show a pair of strange, clear eyes—like quartz that had seen fire.

"I'm not meant to ride," he said. "But I was meant to meet *you*."

Beck's grip tightened on the wheel.

"Who are you?"

"I'm called Miles. I walk between places most people forget. The trees told me you'd be coming."

Hattie leaned closer. "Do you know where we're going?"

Miles gave the faintest smile. "Not precisely. But I know what you'll find when you get there. They've been hurt. But before that..."

He reached into his coat and pulled out something wrapped in faded cloth. He handed it to Hattie, who handed it to Beck.

Beck unwrapped it. A chunk of tree root, carved into the shape of a sleeping fox.

"The Sequoias gave me that," Miles said. "They said you'd know what to do with it when the time comes."

Beck stared at it, his throat tight.

"And me?" Hattie asked.

"You'll be asked to trust something that makes no sense. You'll be tempted to say no. Don't."

Then, without another word, Miles turned and walked into the trees lining the road and vanished. The forest closed back around him.

Hattie looked at Beck nervously. "Well... that wasn't ominous at *all*."

Beck held the fox root, examining it.

"The Sequoia trees have been wounded. They know something. I think we're going to need this soon."

The van rolled forward, deeper into the unknown. The road narrowed as the van climbed into the hills, the trees growing taller and thicker on either side, oak giving way to fir, then pine, then to redwood. The air grew heavier. Not hot, but *dense*, like the sky had lowered a little. Beck turned off the radio.

Not that it had been playing anything—just static and short bursts of sound. He slowed to a crawl. Hattie leaned forward, squinting.

"Beck... does the road look different to you?"

He nodded. "It's too straight."

The road *was* perfectly straight. A ribbon of asphalt, perfectly flat, cutting through a forest that had no business letting it exist. No curves, no dips. Just a clean line stretching on and on.

And the trees...

They weren't swaying.

Not even a little bit.

Beck stopped the van. They got out. The silence wrapped around them like heavy wet wool. No wind. No birds. No insects. Just... *stillness.*

Beck went to the nearest redwood and laid his hand against its bark. Normally, he would feel the low thrum of memory, sap-thoughts, root-rumors. But now. Nothing. No voice. No history.

Hattie stepped to the edge of the road, where an abandoned shack leaned crooked under the weight of vines. It hadn't been there a minute ago.

She frowned. "This place is whispering wrong."

Beck turned. "What do you mean?"

Hattie touched the side of the rickety shack, pressing her palm to the wood. Her eyes fluttered shut. Then—she gasped.

"Beck—this house is *new.*"

He stared. "That's not possible."

"No memories," she said. "No dust in the walls. No heat lines. It *looks* old, but it's pretending."

Beck stepped back from the tree. "So are the redwoods. Fake."

They stood still, surrounded by perfect stillness, on a road that didn't bend and under trees that didn't breathe and a house that wasn't there.

Then, from far down the road behind them, a single crow called once—loud and sudden. And the silence *cracked.* The wind returned. The trees exhaled. The road shimmered and bent slightly, as if something had relaxed its grip. The shack was gone.

Hattie turned slowly. "I think we just passed through something. Something testing us."

Beck didn't answer. He was staring at the carved fox in his hand. It had begun to *glow.* Just faintly. Just enough to remind them to get going.

That night, they camped in a small clearing off the side of the road, nestled among a ring of twisted trees with smooth, peeling bark that glowed softly in the moonlight. They built a small fire, cooked beans, and split a square of dark chocolate Hattie had been saving since Arizona. The air had shifted again—less eerie, more expectant.

Beck fell asleep first, one hand still resting on the carved fox. Hattie stayed up a little longer, humming a tune to the trees, whispering thanks to the roots for not pulling away. She crawled into her bedroll beside Beck and slept, wrapped in a patchwork quilt that smelled like old lavender and road dust.

Hattie dreamed. In her dream, she stood on the doorstep of a massive house—too big to be real, too familiar to be imagined. The door was open, but the inside was shifting. Walls moved like breath. Floors bent like old promises.

She stepped inside. Every room was different. One was filled with wind. Another with weeping. One held her childhood rocking chair, but when she reached for it, it crumbled into sand.

And then—The *kitchen*. Clean. Bright. A window looking out into a forest of redwood pillars, taller than cathedrals. Someone was sitting at the table. A woman with hair made of twisting ivy, skin like cracked plaster, and a long, crooked smile that almost reached kindness.

"I've been waiting," the woman said. Her voice sounded like creaking stairs. "You're late, little House Whisperer."

Hattie stepped closer, heart pounding. "Who are you?"

"I am the Dreamline's ghost," the woman said.

"The memory of what's been kept too long. I know your name and your silliness. And I know you'll be asked to trust something impossible soon. Better quit gabbing, listen and say yes."

The dream shattered. Hattie sat up with a gasp, heart thudding, breath shallow. Beck was already awake, kneeling beside the fire, staring at the fox carving. It was glowing again.

Beck reached out his hand.

"We're close."

By late afternoon, the road gave way to dirt. The van couldn't go any further. They left it tucked beneath a low canopy of trees and hiked the rest of the way on foot.

They reached the grove near dusk, the sky behind them bruised with lavender and fire. The air was thick with the scent of ash and pine sap, and the Sequoias—those mighty sentinels—stood oddly silent.

Not reverent.

Not peaceful.

Just... watching.

The carved fox in Beck's hand pulsed warm and steady, guiding them. The redwoods rose around them, impossibly tall, impossibly still. They looked around. The grove had no welcome sign, no markings, no fence.

Light filtered down like liquid gold, silent and sacred. The trunks of the redwoods stood like ancient gods, their roots coiled and sunken, their bark etched with time.

Beck dropped to one knee, placed the fox carving on a patch of soft earth. Hattie, her boots crunching over charred needles and broken branches wandered father into the grove. Beck followed, walking softly as if approaching an injured animal.

"I feel it," he said. "Something's wrong."

They moved deeper into the grove. Then they saw it. A great tree at the grove's heart—burned from the inside out. Its bark split and blackened, its branches twisted like they'd tried to wrench themselves away from the pain. The wound wasn't from lightning or fire alone—it pulsed with hate.

Hattie dropped to her knees, her hand pressed to the scorched ground.

"It wasn't just fire," she whispered. "It was *Hate*. Someone brought destruction here on purpose."

Beck knelt beside her. He pressed both palms to the roots and closed his eyes. "The trees are still linked... barely. But the network's frayed. This wound blocks the flow. Until it's healed, the light can't pass between this point and New Mexico."

"We're the bridge," Hattie said. "We must be."

She pulled out a worn roll of cloth—tools, chalk, and dried herbs she hadn't known why she'd packed until now.

"We'll need a house blessing. And whatever you do with your tree whispering."

Beck smiled grimly. "I'll ask them what they remember. And what they're willing to let go of."

Together, they began the work. Hattie whispered prayers in a forgotten tongue, drawing protection symbols in the dirt. Beck chanted softly to the roots, coaxing them to remember wind and rain, kindness and quiet.

Night fell. A faint shimmer began to rise from the wounded tree—like moonlight through a cracked door.

Then came a sound. Low. Deep. Felt more in the bones than heard in the ears. A voice—not words exactly, but *intent*. Ancient. Measured. Beck translated aloud, his voice shaking:

"This grove remembers the first lattice. It held the western edge while the veil was young. But we have been starving. Hidden. Forgotten. You bring the breath back. You bring the bond."

Hattie stepped forward.

"What do we do next?"

Silence. The fox carving crumbled into dust. A single redwood root pushed gently upward, curling toward Beck's hand.

He touched it.

The ground pulsed once.

And far away, in the desert store, the copper disk under Avery's altar flickered briefly with red light—then stilled.

The western point had just stirred.

Not fully awakened.

Wounded, but no longer alone...

Hattie and Beck worked non-stop-practically, magically, and soul-first—to awaken and anchor the Western Guardian Point of Light, the redwood grove. Beck palmed the bark of the redwood trees, one by one, letting each redwood "speak" its memories. Each spoke of fires survived, rains withheld, logging scars, and children who once hid inside burned-out hollows. He mapped those memories like rings.

Hattie walked the invisible "rooms" of the grove—the clearings, the paths, the nurse logs, the fallen giants, treating them as a house without walls. She learned where the "kitchen warmth" was, the hearth, the "basement," root tangles holding the redwoods sorrows, the "attic" where whispers became voices, and the "front porch," the threshold where the veil thinned.

Beck sketched a root map in the soil with charcoal and crushed fern, aligning the oldest mother tree to true north. Hattie marked the thresholds with bundles of cedar, sage, and old nails she carried for "house-speaking"—not to nail things shut, but to ground the edges of the Good so the Good could stay and the hungry couldn't take.

Together, they made four small altars at the edges of the grove in the four directions. Then Beck sang to them in tree language.

Low and slow, the sounds like sap moving, Beck used silence that sounded like foghorns and whales. Suddenly, the grove began to pulse in sync with the Desert Store (south) and the Timmon's Tower (north). Tiny red-gold motes rose like dust motes in the dancing Light. The lattice was remembering.

At night, so they couldn't be seen, so the copper wires wound around the trees could stay magnetized, by campfire light, they braided the copper wire with thin, redwood roots and laid more of the living circuit out in the four directions. When it was finished, Beck and Hattie placed both their palms on the conductors and spoke the Keepers Call. The copper and tree roots answered.

In New Mexico, Avery's copper disk flashed green for the first time. In Colorado, Timmon's gemstones vibrated—not visibly, but Gordon felt it in his molars and swore softly, smiling. The western point of light was awake again.

Chapter Seven: Shem Rickleman

Shem Rickleman was still walking—had been for months. Maybe years if you counted all the false starts and roundabout loops. The Carolina coast wasn't a place he'd planned to end up. He wasn't sure he'd planned anything at all. But his feet knew something his mind didn't, and every sunrise came up with him slightly farther east.

Shem was a Walker. Not just a man who walked—but someone *tuned* to the walking rhythm of all things traveling. He'd watched the way wind leaned through wheat fields. The way fence lines bowed after a hard winter. The way waterways argued with roads. He could *feel* the pull of his next step before it landed.

Orphaned at twelve, he'd been on the road ever since. His mother had vanished in the night—fleeing an abusive man and the wreckage of boys just like him. She left behind a duffel bag of canned peaches, three dollars in change, and one whispered truth:

"Shem, he's not your real daddy. You look for the one with the green-colored eyes."

Then she was gone. Shem had been looking for her ever since. Not just for her. Not just for the man with the green-colored eyes. But for a place that would *stop pulling* long enough for him to rest.

He was too hairy and too short, and too wiry and lean, with dust in his seams and a scar over his left eyebrow that twitched when rain was predicted. Folks passed him on roads and thought he was just another rough-soul wanderer and dismissed him.

But there was plenty more to him. He had inherited his mother's Sight. A flicker in the corner of his eye when he passed certain crossroads. A prickle in his spine when certain birds flew too low. A dormant Sight, inherited from his mother, curled like smoke beneath his ribs. He didn't understand it. Didn't try to. He just kept walking.

He was headed to the Carolina coast. Not for the ocean. Not for the sunrises. He was being *drawn* there. Drawn by dreams of a Sleeping Woman who breathed in rhythm with the tide. Drawn by whispers of a rebirth of Light. He didn't know it yet. But he knew she was waiting for him. And that his world would change forever when he found her...

Shem Rickleman arrived at the odd little Carolina coast town at twilight. He didn't know the name of the town. Or if it even *was* a town anymore. A few sun-bleached houses slouched behind a dune ridge, shutters loose, porches half-swallowed by salt grass. No one stirred. The air smelled of seaweed, rust, and memory.

He stepped up his pace through town, then follow the wind down a narrow path, his worn boots kicking through soft sand and crushed oyster shell. After awhile, the dunes opened to a wide stretch of marsh and beyond it—a dock.

Old. Rotted. Abandoned. The kind of dock no one fished from anymore. The dock jutted crooked into the water like a broken finger pointing east toward the deeper dark. Planks warped, sea-worn ropes dangling like forgotten thoughts.

Shem knew it was *the right place.* Not because he'd seen it in a dream. Not because his Sight told him. When he stepped onto the first board, the hair on his arms stood up. The wind stopped. He inched forward, boots moving soft and cautious on ancient wood. Halfway down the dock, he stopped. The sea stretched out in front of him like a sleeping animal. Quiet. Alive.

He dropped to one knee and placed his hand flat on the wood. It was warm. Not from sun. From *presence.* A pulse. Low. Slow. Like breath. Far out in the water, the tide shifted. A swell rose. A single wave moved toward the shore—*not crashing,* just folding like a heartbeat coming home. The dock swayed beneath him.

Shem dropped to the deck. He sat on the dock long after the light faded. The tide whispered below him, lapping gently at the worn pilings. He sat with his legs dangling over the edge, boots off, bare feet in the brine, toes curling into the water's rhythm like they belonged there. Because they did.

Shem had always been a water dog. A swimmer from the start. He remembered long days as a boy, before everything fell apart—splashing in muddy creeks, floating belly-up in swimming holes, fishing in silence with his mama beside him, their bare knees touching, her quiet smile doing more good than words ever could.

The loves of his life had always been his mother and all forms of water. He could watch a fountain endlessly. He knew the frogs and bogs and sullen waves of many shores from his travels.

He could read a current like a book. Feel a storm two days out just by the way the pelicans flew. And he *loved* it. Not just water—but what it *did*. The way it remembered. The way it forgave. The way it didn't explain itself. He thought about the mysterious ways of water as he trailed his fingers in the shallows...

While the man dozed, as if in a trance, Marisong studied him thoroughly, hungrily, from her mist drenched, hidden boat and learned him. They called her the Sleeping Woman. Other men had tried to find her before him. They walked the dunes. Stood at the edge of her salt-breathing world. But none of them *loved* the water. Not the way this man did. They came with fear, or power, or prophecy. Greedy for ownership, not *kinship*.

He was a water man. And that was what she had been waiting for. A kindred pulse. A swimmer. This man was kin. She began to willingly awake from her dream state. Not suddenly. Not like thunder. But like fog rolling slowly back across a still morning.

Shem awoke. He felt something—not in his bones, but in the way the air curved around him. The tide pulled *in*, rather than out. The dock creaked like it was remembering something. A light—not from the moon—glimmered beneath the water's surface. A voice—not words, not sound, but *water knowing*—bubbled up into his chest: "Waterman."

Shem whispered back, not sure if the whisper came from his head or in his mouth: "I didn't come to wake you. I came to find my mother."

The water shifted. Startled, Shem pulled his feet from the water and sat very still. The tide lapped below, whispering its strange, wordless invitation. He felt it calling—not with urgency, but with *recognition.* A pull as old as his bones.

But Shem Rickleman was not a man of impulse. Years on the road had carved impulsiveness out of him. He was caution itself. Caution had kept him breathing when a storm rolled across a highway in the dark. Or when he slept in rough out way. Caution had kept him alive when he slept under bridges, when every shadow could be a thief or killer or worse. Some of those had tried to take him out. He sat there, *thinking.* Remembering his mother's voice. Her warnings. Her quiet strength.

The water hummed softly, as if waiting, pulling at him to come on in. Shem stood up. His boots scuffed the worn boards as he backed away from the edge of the dock. It wasn't time. Not yet. Off the dock, he turned back toward the path on the dunes.

Not far from the dock, he saw the cabin. It was half-hidden by vines and moonlight. A small cabin. Wood grayed by the salt air, its front porch steps sagging, but not unfriendly. A faint candle flickered in the window. He hesitated a minute before walking closer. He stood in the yard, staring at the cabin.

The door creaked open, and an old woman stood there, her hair a tangle of white and gray, her shawl covered in little shells that clinked when she moved. Shem froze. Not in fear. In *recognition.* He didn't know her. But in some deep way, she knew him.

"Come on in, boy," she said, voice steady and warm as tidewater. "You've walked far enough tonight."

And just like that—Shem, who trusted almost nothing all of his life—felt *safe.* As if he had stepped into a story his mother had left behind for him long ago. Shem found himself in the presence of both his ancestry and destiny.

The old woman's cabin smelled of salt, cedar, and something warm on the stove—maybe sassafras or molasses. It was dim inside, lit only by a single lamp and a tangle of dried herbs hanging from the rafters.

Shem sat near the fire, hat in his lap, unsure if he should speak first. The old woman poured tea into a mismatched cup and handed it to him without asking how he liked it. She knew.

"You're not the first to come," she said, settling into a worn rocker. "But you might be the first one to stay."

Shem looked up. "I didn't mean to come here. I was just walking. Looking."

The old woman smiled, her eyes sharp as sea glass. "And what were you looking for?"

"My mother," he said softly. "And maybe... something I lost when she left."

She nodded, as if she'd heard that kind of grief before. "She was right to tell you who your father was. Green-colored eyes aren't a common thing. But they're a *marker.* And they show up when the water's getting ready to shift."

Shem blinked. "You knew her?"

"I know *you,* child." She looked toward the window, where moonlight laced the curtains like netting. They both stood still as statues and the knowing in each of them deepened. She finally sighed and said, "You're one of ours. You've got that ripple in your blood. You hear what others miss. You walk when others stop. You *feel* tide before it rises. You know about water."

Shem swallowed. "Who are you?"

"I'm her grandmother," the woman said simply. "The one out in the boat."

Shem turned sharply. "What boat?"

The woman rose and opened the cabin door. She pointed out past the dunes, beyond the marsh, to where the water lay still as glass. There, just barely visible in the moonlight, rocked a small wooden boat. A shape inside. Sleeping. Covered in sea-green cloth.

"The Sleeping Woman," the old woman said. "My granddaughter. Marisong. She is dreaming the tides right now. She'll wake when the Light fully returns. Or when someone who speaks the water gives her reason to."

Shem felt his throat tighten. He didn't believe in fate. But he knew pull when he felt it. He stepped onto the porch, heart pounding, the tide inside him matching the tide outside.

"She'll know you by your silence first," the old woman said behind him. "And maybe, if it's meant to be, by your love after that."

Shem turned. "Love?"

The old woman smiled. "She needs someone who can both walk and swim. Someone who knows both the road and the current. Someone with a scar from both."

And Shem—wiry, weatherworn, carrying half a lifetime of ache—realized maybe he hadn't just been looking for his mother all this time. Maybe he'd been looking for his true *home*.

And maybe she was out there—sleeping in a boat, breathing in rhythm with the sea, waiting for him to be *ready*.

His life had suddenly become a deep, quiet fairytale with sea air in its lungs. A sleeping beauty of the tides, a tide-worn traveler, and a grandmother with years tucked into her shawl. He needed their names and to let himself settle in to this situation. Healing would take time. Waking from a dream like this might take longer. He suspected he might have to tarry here a long time.

The old woman's name was Miz Windletta March, though she told Shem just to call her *Miz Wind*.

"Folks forget the 'letta' part anyway," she said, stirring sassafras into her tea. "Wind" will do fine. That's what I've always answered to. Wind—that's what has always carried her boat home."

Her granddaughter, the Sleeping Woman, was named Marisong.

"It means sea song," Miz Wind said, watching him. "Her mama was wild about naming her something that would never settle. Said the sea would raise her, and one day the sea would send someone back to her."…

Shem, bone-tired and soul-scattered, stayed. He didn't mean to. He told himself he'd just rest a few nights. Get his bearings. Maybe mend his worn out boots and move on. Instead, he mended the porch steps.

Helped Miz Wind patch the roof after a sudden storm rattled across it. Cleaned the stone well behind the house, tossed the vines into a fire he'd made.

He kept on working, making Miz Wind's place tidy and welcoming like he pictured a home should be. After a while, he stopped counting the days. Stopped wondering when he'd leave. He noted the rhythm of tide and sea and slept long and deep for the first time in years. He rested and learned.

Marisong remained asleep in her boat, just offshore, tucked in her sea-colored blanket. The boat never drifted, never sank. It bobbed gently night and day. A quiet pulse on the water. Sometimes, at dawn, Shem swore he saw her hand move. Once, at dusk, he thought she smiled. But Miz Wind shook her head.

"Not yet," she'd say softly. "She's listening still. Not to words. To just *being*. It's what she needs. And what you need, too."

Shem chopped wood. Fished. Sat on the dock some evenings and played his mother's old harmonica. Not songs—just notes. Whistles of feeling. The kind the sea might understand. And day by day, Shem Rickleman—the Walker, the lost son— began to settle. Not into stillness. But into *place*. Into Miz Wind's world. Into something rooted.

He didn't know it yet, but Marisong could hear him. Not in sound—but in sea-tone and shore-thought. She was beginning to remember the shape of his voice and the rhythm of the one who had *come to stay.*

Miz Wind didn't talk much about the past. Not at first. She lived in the now—tea kettle boiling, tide chart chalked on the wall, herbs drying like old flags above the window.

One cool evening, after Shem had fixed the porch screen and split a stack of driftwood logs, she brought out an old photo wrapped in oilcloth. It showed a woman wild-eyed and beautiful, barefoot in the marsh grass, holding a baby close to her chest.

"That was my daughter," Miz Wind said, her voice as thin as a gull's cry. "And that's Marisong."

She didn't sit as she spoke. She stayed standing, back straight, looking out toward the sea.

"My daughter, Lessa, was born with too much wind in her bones. She wanted to fly. Always said the sea would never own her, that roots were for cowards. First chance she got, she ran. Took up with a man who liked potions more than promises. Followed storms instead of shelter."

Miz Wind turned to Shem. "She left Marisong here with me when she was just three. Said she'd come back. Said she just needed time. She never came back."

Shem didn't speak. He didn't need to. He'd heard the same promise from his own mother before she vanished into the long road, leaving him behind.

"She wrote one letter," Miz Wind said softly, "from some city far away. Said she'd found herself. Said she hoped I'd forgive her. Said Marisong was better off."

She closed her eyes. "I did forgive her. But Marisong never forgot. She waited on that dock every morning for weeks. Wouldn't let me brush her hair. Said Mama would want to do it."

Shem's throat tightened.

"She waited so long, she stopped waiting. Then she went to sleep-slept." Miz Wind's voice cracked. "And she hasn't woken all this time. Not truly. She walks in dreams. And I keep her safe in the boat because the sea still sings to her, and the sea hasn't given her back to me yet."

Shem stood, the harmonica in his pocket feeling heavier now.

"I know what that kind of waiting does," he said finally.

Miz Wind nodded sympathetically. "That's why you're here." They didn't speak more that night.

But something had shifted with their words. Two abandoned children—now grown—finding in each other a mirrored sorrow. And out in the boat, Marisong stirred in her sleep. Not ready to wake. But beginning to dream of someone who *stayed*.

Day after day passed, like pearls sliding off a thread. Shem stayed. He mended the fence around the herb garden, repaired the stone steps that led to the spring, added a second chair to the porch without saying why. Beneath his steady hands, something rare began to form—not just a place to rest, but a foundation strong enough for his Sight to rise and shine. He didn't know how to force it. Didn't try. He just listened. To the sea. To the wind. To the hush between Miz Wind's sentences.

And while he rooted himself, the Sleeping Woman began to stir. Marisong was no longer just a shape beneath a blanket on the boat. One morning, Shem noticed the boat was tied to the dock—softly swaying, empty. After that, things changed, but never loudly. He'd come back from fishing and find a teacup rinsed and turned upside down on the drying mat. A sweater missing from the hook by the door. A second bowl of soup gone by morning.

Marisong had begun slipping in and out of the cabin like sea mist—no footsteps, no door creak, no announcement. Just signs. A soft robe drying on the line. Wet hair glistening in the sink. A forgotten lemon wedge on the cutting board. She was waking. Becoming human again. But she kept to herself, like a tide not ready to come in.

Neither Shem nor Miz Wind spoke of it. Not directly. Because they knew—Marisong could hear whispers from afar. So Shem carried on with his work in silence. And Miz Wind only hummed now and then as she stirred her pots. They shared an unspoken agreement. No prodding. No questions. Let her come back in her own time.

But every now and then, Shem would glance at the dock, at the boat tied fast, and feel a thread of anticipation tug in his chest. She was there. Not just dreaming now. Not just a ghost of the water. She was walking the edges of waking. And something in her was watching, listening, beginning to trust.

One gray-blue morning, Shem came in from hauling driftwood and paused at the door. Something was different. The air inside the cabin held a hush, like it had just finished speaking. He stepped in slowly, boots quiet on the floorboards.

Miz Wind was nowhere in sight—probably down by the marsh, tending her clamshell traps. But on the table... a folded piece of paper, held in place by a smooth black water stone. The paper was pale, edged with salt-stiff corners. His name was written on the front in careful, slightly shaky handwriting. Just, Shem.

Shem sat down, hands rough from rope and wood, and opened it. "I remember your voice. Not from words, but from the quiet. You don't press. You don't pull. You wait. That's why I can hear you. Sometimes, I wake in the middle of the night and know you're outside, thinking. You are like a steady lighthouse in the dark. I don't know how to be back... *in the world* yet. But I'll leave the boat soon. Not today. Maybe not tomorrow. But soon. Remember, the side room and its door are mine. I shall come and go without questions. —M"

Shem held the note for a long time. Then he placed it back beneath the black stone, rose, and quietly set a second cup beside his own on the porch railing. Just in case.

Chapter Eight: Place them Straight

Avery, William, and Lily Jean Bloome sat out back, under a quilt of stars, their fingers aching from the day's work. Coils of hammered copper lay stacked beside them, glinting orange in the firelight. Spun into spirals, loops, and lattices, the shapes felt half-ancient, half-future. None of them could explain exactly *why* they had spent the whole day shaping copper into strange curves and coils—but they had done it anyway, as if some part of them remembered a purpose the mind hadn't yet caught up to.

"It's like weaving music out of metal," William said earlier, wiping sweat from his brow.

Avery nodded. "Or spinning protection."

Lily Jean Bloome, who had made the most delicate pieces of all, leaned back against a sun-bleached barrel, her braid trailing over one shoulder.

"We'll know what they're for when it's time," she said softly, sipping cactus blossom tea.

The wind murmured through the desert grasses. Avery stared into the fire, shoulders loose but eyes sharp. "There's something coming," he said, not with dread, but with certainty. "I can feel it."

"We all can," she agreed. William stretched his legs out and sighed. "Good thing we've got copper. And guts. And an old truck that still runs."

They laughed—tired but grounded. No one mentioned the Light that had started to pulse again in the northern sky. No one spoke of the dreams that had returned, filled with signs, symbols, and visitors who spoke in riddles.

Instead, they sat together in silence, the good kind, surrounded by the warmth of fire, friendship, and something unnamed but sacred.

The wind began to whisper low over the desert brush. They felt a soft presence come to rest behind them. Startled, William turned first. And there she stood. Emma. A commanding, lithe, swaying presence. Emma. His daughter. Small framed, thin and petite, elegant even in the shadows, she stood framed in the back doorway of the desert store, one hand lightly braced against the wood, the other hand holding the handle of her smart and discreet leather satchel. Her hair was slightly out of place, but not much, her large dark eyes rimmed with fatigue.

She'd flown home from Spain, urged on by dreams that would not let her be. Dreams that told her *he*—William—was in the middle of something vast and urgent. Dreams that whispered her name over desert sands. She'd left her husband behind with a kiss and no promises of a timely return. He let her go-offered to join her. But no—this was hers alone to do.

Emma was the toast of Europe—*a world-famous artist* who painted in vast, wild swaths of color that had left critics gasping. Primitive, visceral, untamed. And yet, she hadn't touched a brush in months. Not since she was called to the monastery to paint the Three Magi's Inner Fears. Her paintings had set them free. And she had finally understood that from then on, sometimes her paintings would not be about her. They would be about others. And belong to them. Terrified at the gift she'd discovered, she stopped painting. Ah yes- there was once- in a dream state, she had painted a demon away from a Traveler. That had frightened her even more.

She started down the back steps to join them, her boots stirring the dust, accepting whatever her part was in what was coming.

Then she saw Avery. Her face blanched. William raced to grab her before she fainted. The flames caught the faint shimmer of paint still lingering on her fingertips—ghosts of color not yet born.

Avery froze as Emma's knees buckled. His heart slammed against his ribs, his mouth suddenly dry. The copper spinner he'd been holding clattered to the ground, forgotten. He moved forward slowly, like he was approaching a flame that could burn or bless. William caught Emma just before she collapsed, his arms around her like the past trying to shield the future.

Avery's voice came out rough, unused. "Emma...?"

She blinked up at him, breath shallow. Her fingers trembled in William's grip.

"You're dead," she whispered, the words cracking under the weight of disbelief. "We buried you."

"I know," Avery said, taking another step. His voice steadied. "I didn't stay dead."

He reached for her hand, hesitated, then gently took it. The faint shimmer of paint on her fingertips passed onto his skin like a blessing. Or a curse. She didn't pull away.

"I came back because I wasn't done," he said softly. "And neither are you."

Emma let out a long, shaky breath and sighed.

No one said anything more for a long while. The desert wind danced through the fire, whispering stories not yet finished. Something big was about to begin.

A few nights later, Emma sat in the firelight, her eyes clear and steady as they moved from William to Avery, then back to Lily Jean Bloome.

"I dreamed copper," she said. Four heads turned toward her. "I dreamed all your hands spinning it. And I saw Shadows trying to escape it. I didn't know why then. But now I do. You're to put the copper in the ground. It is a conductor.

"Lily Jean Bloome will map it for you. Most of the copper will be placed out with the red cacti so they can expand their "eating" of negative energies. Every Point of Light is making copper underground "grids," though they don't look like grids, to connect to each other.

"I'm here to paint the bad things for you," she said. Her voice didn't tremble.

No one spoke right away. Avery tilted his head, something flickering behind his eyes—recognition, maybe. Lily' Jean Bloome's breath caught, just slightly. William blinked, then gave the smallest nod, as if something unspoken between them had just fallen into place. Emma looked at the copper coils piled at their feet and reached out to touch one.

"You can't always name the dark," she said softly. "But you can paint it. And then the light knows where to land."

She unbuckled the worn satchel she carried and laid it down by the fire.

The brushes inside hadn't been touched in months, but they gleamed faintly, like they'd been waiting.

"I won't ask questions," she added. "I don't need to know the whole story. Just the shape of what's coming. The story has to be told in the dark, then carried into the Light."

She sat cross-legged near the fire, pulled out a piece of canvas rolled tight like a scroll.

She unrolled the canvas with slow hands, her fingers trembling slightly as if they already knew what they were about to summon. She looked up at the others—firelight flickering in her eyes, reflecting not fear, but a terrible clarity.

"I'm here to paint the bad things for you," she said again. "But they'll try to destroy me. And they might succeed before I can finish. So you must protect me."

Silence dropped heavy, the kind that wraps around the bones.

"They always come," she said, eyes distant with prophecy. "When truth starts to take form—when the shape of evil is revealed—they *come*. Shadows. False voices. People who aren't people. They'll slip through dreams, through cracks in time, through mirrors if they have to."

William moved toward her instinctively, protectively, but Emma raised a hand.

"It's all right, Dad. I knew before I came. The dream said: *Your brushes will bleed. Your hands will burn. But someone has to show them what's coming.*"...

They heard a shout.

"Well, Dumbasses, you're not going to fight a war alone! I love a good fight!"

Their beloved Normaine who had lived at the store for years, scarred, one-eyed, and formidable, a hefty Native American artist who forged metal into magic sounds and shapes, came stomping down the back steps like a storm wrapped in denim and dust. Behind her trailed her suave and laid back husband, Eddy, a dapper little Italian ex-semi driver with a crooked grin and road miles still in his bones.

"By God, you're not going to go into battle without me and Eddy! You should have told us! Dumbasses!" she shouted her favorite word. Jabbing a calloused finger towards the fire, she shouted, "I'll make metal you can *hold* anything off with. Shields. Bangles. Armor, if need be. No one's gonna' take out my people while I'm still breathing!"

She grinned. "And I can hammer too. I still got muscle in these arms besides love in my heart for my sweetheart, honey bun, baby cakes Eddy! Besides, the mobiles I make? They don't just spin pretty. I wire 'em to sing when evil's nearby. They'll sort out every single movement in the air. Like chimes on the wind—except they *warn*. We got 'em, I tell ya!" Normaine crowed, planting her fists on her hips. "Let the bastards come."

Emma blinked, then laughed—just once. A burst of surprised gratitude caught in her throat. She wiped the corner of her eye with the back of her sleeve.

"Thank you," she whispered.

Normaine stepped closer, her rough hand clapping Emma's shoulder. "You paint. We'll cover your back."

Avery stood up, standing beside Emma, while William and Eddy hugged. Lily Jean Bloome walked over to them, one hand pressed to her heart, the other already beginning a soft chant of protection. And above them all, the quilt of stars blinked down as if listening in.

Normaine was still ranting about forging metal into holy hellfire when Eddy, rolling his shoulders with the slow ease of an ex-trucker who'd once hauled both dreams and demons across countless state lines, cracked his knuckles and said with his crooked smile that only Normaine ever fully trusted,

"I'll drive 'em to the edge of hell and drop 'em off myself," Eddy nodded. "Yep. Justified. That's right. That's us. I've got diesel in my veins and an old road map burned into my bones. If they're coming for us, I'll meet 'em halfway and leave their sorry shadows crying on the curb."

Normaine gave a whoop. "That's my man!" she shouted.

Lily grinned. "Well, they're not ready for you, Eddy."

"I know," he said. "Ain't nobody ever ready for a long-hauler's tough love story."

The laughter that followed was short, sharp, and needed. Emma smiled, just barely. Then she said, "All right then. Let's get to work."

Normaine sat down beside Avery, her denim jacket creaking as she shifted her weight onto the stump.

The fire crackled behind them, sending up little sparks like impatient questions waiting for answers. She didn't hesitate.

"I thought I'd seen me a ghost when I saw you from the porch. Me and Eddy," she said, her voice low and thick with emotion. "What happened to you?"

She didn't wait for his reply. Her composure cracked open like dry earth meeting rain. A choked sob escaped her lips, and she reached out, wrapping her strong arms around Avery, pulling him close like she was trying to piece back together everything that had ever gone missing in her life.

"I thought you were dead all this time," she whispered, her voice muffled against his shoulder. "We all did. We didn't even look for you," she said, in a voice filled with both wonder and guilt.

Avery didn't speak right away. His jaw tightened, and his hands rested awkwardly in his lap, as though unsure what to do with the weight of her grief. Eddy, standing nearby with his arms crossed and his eyes shining, finally said. "We all need to know, Avery."

Emma stcppcd forward from thc shadows, hcr arms wrapped around herself. "Please," she added softly, "it's time."

Avery looked from face to face, his eyes lingering on each of them—their worry, their loyalty, their quiet hope. Then he exhaled slowly, like something inside him finally gave way. The truth was dark and heavy. Maybe they wouldn't believe him. But it was time to tell it. He glanced toward the fire, then back at the beloveds who had waited, hoped, and suffered.

"Alright," he said hoarsely, "I'll tell you everything I remember, but I'll make it short."

He took a long breath. Then, without flourish or apology, he spoke.

"A flying beast the size of a small dragon with a spade tail whipping back and forth, came out of the air and pierced me through the heart. It was black with a red tail. It poisoned me, and I passed out. Next thing I know, I was in an ambulance. Sirens. They took me to a compound in a desert. A Keeper ran it. An old weird shaped thing. Eyes like smoke. They put me in a cell. Locked me up. Drugs. No clock. No sky. Years passed, I think. I counted heartbeats just to stay alive.

Then one day, something shifted, and I knew someone was coming for me. Someone Good. The place was suddenly deserted. My cell door stood open. I managed to get out and into the compound. Timmon's father saved me. Then Timmon and William drove me back here. To my home."

With that said, he was done. The fire popped, the copper wires hummed, and the wind around the desert store changed direction as if the world itself had just taken notice...

At the desert store, they worked together again, each in their own way, to strengthen the Points of Light. Normaine returned to her old ways, hammering out metal mobiles and hanging them everywhere—on the front and back porch, everywhere—letting them catch the wind and sing like they used to when she lived at the desert store.

Normaine tuned into frequencies only she could hear, and rebalanced each mobile to a purpose she instinctively knew.

Eddy polished and tuned every moving part he could find of anything, muttering to bolts and wheels as he coaxed speed back into them. Lily Jean Bloome spread her maps across # 1 motel room wall, tracking ancient lines and lay paths, eyes flickering with patterns only she could see.

William kept his Sight fixed on distant omens, calmly watching the horizon for what might come next.

Avery stayed steady at the center of it all, instructing those who arrived—quiet souls drawn by the pull of something old and true.

They were Light Workers now, all of them. Together, they moved into the motel behind the desert store and waited. The air shifted. The ground knew. And somewhere in the silence between the stars above, and the waiting ones below, the war between Evil and Good, Darkness and Light, tilted ever so slightly towards Hope...

Elsewhere, things were happening to four other people who accidentally- so they thought-had once fought a psychic battle at the desert store and won. Susan Sugar Diamond, Matthew Judson, Perry Judson, and Lana English were being nudged by Light-once more-without understanding why. All four of them were beautiful, rich, and stubborn, so Light was having quite a time getting them to pay attention.

They wandered the world together, still claiming the Good versus Evil battle they'd been a part of back at the desert store was just a coincidence—but finally they began to wonder.

They flew back to America, got a van, began driving, pulling off of highways without knowing why. They stopped at motels, diners, abandoned gas stations. Looked them over. Studied the air, the ground, the buildings, the trees and plants growing nearby. They bought books on plants and studied them. None of the four had ever been interested in plants.

They shook their heads in both irritation and wonder, but kept on going. Each place they stopped at was once a Light chakra, though none of them realized that. They only knew they felt... settled there. In out of the way, homely, neglected places. They stayed for a short time in each one. Like something unseen had waved them in, done something to them, then sent them on their way again...

Back in Carolina, Geena and her daughter Celia kept waking at night to the same sound: a woman's voice, singing low, calling to them to solve a mystery that came from the sea. Pulled from their sleep and rest, they trekked to the coast. Geena gassed up the 1959 Dodge Lancer and they packed what they needed into her beloved old land yacht.

"This car has always had character," Geena said, running her fingers across the lines above the taillights. "And something special, I don't know what. It's still in tip top condition."

"Come on, Mama!' Celia said. "Let's go!"

Geena grinned at Celia.

"Okay. Just like old times, eh, kiddo?"

"Yeah. But this time we're not running away from home. We're just going to find out what the hell is disturbing our usual prim and prissy little lives."

They both laughed as Geena rolled out of the driveway with her husband Ray Makepeace, big boss of his home, errant father and womanizer, glaring from the living room window of their mansion with disapproval.

Celia loved her father but had started calling him *Ray*—his first name—after she'd discovered his countless brief affairs. Affairs that, by some miracle, hadn't yet gotten him sued or fired from his position as a big shot professor with tenure at the nearby university. Celia knew Geena knew. But they never spoke of it.

Celia thought about Timmon. She'd been in love with him since they met at the Desert Store, back when she was just a kid with scraped knees twirling a sword made of driftwood. Her thoughts wrapped around him now with the same fierce pull they always had, stretching across time and spacc like a tether.

They kept driving. They didn't know they were searching for an old, deserted sea town with the Eastern Point of Light hidden somewhere near it...

Far away, the young man known as Timmon to Celia—Crowell G. Restus II, son of another world Undertaker, Crowell Restus 1—suddenly paused in his work. He tilted his head, as if catching a scent on the wind.

He scowled. "Celia! Give her an inch, she'll take a mile," he muttered, brushing away the ghost of a memory—or maybe it was the faint trace of Celia's lovely mix of scents that had no business drifting across his Colorado property.

He tried to refocus. There was metal to be spun, copper to be shaped, guardian work to be done. But Celia's presence always came like that: uninvited, impossible to ignore, and tangled in the air like a spell. He shook his head. Went back to work...

They took turns driving. Celia laughed and drove on through the night, the '59 Dodge Lancer rumbling beneath them like a restless dream. Headlights carved soft golden tunnels through the dark as black windfall branches overhead and forgotten signposts flew by.

In the passenger seat, Geena slept the peace of running away—a rare, slack-jawed peace she hadn't known in years. Her head lolled against the passenger window, her hands curled gently in her lap.

Celia glanced at her and softened. "Sleep, Mama," she whispered. "I've got the wheel. You rest. We're running towards something Good again."

The road stretched ahead like a promise, stars spinning above in quiet blessing. Somewhere far behind them, their old life burned itself out. Up ahead lay oceans, awakenings, and whatever waited for women like them who dared to leave and still believed in beginnings.

Chapter Nine: It's Time

Shem Rickleman was following a destiny he didn't yet understand. Four women were gathering by the sea, each with unique abilities, quietly honing their skills for a purpose shrouded in mystery, and he was to be a part of it somehow.

Shem Rickleman had walked far—further than most men ever dared. And now, at the edge of the world, where the land sighed into the ocean, he had found what he didn't know he was seeking: a hidden cabin near the shore, veiled by salt-soaked wind and time.

It was here the old woman, Miz Wind, waited. And in the boat tied to the dock, her granddaughter, Marisong, the sleeping one, stirred.

She wasn't fully awake yet. Not to her power, not to her past, not even to her name. But Shem knew the water whispered to her as it whispered to him.

Miz Wind watched over them both, her eyes as deep as ancient tide pools, holding stories far too old for books. Her hands carried ancestral knowing, and her presence alone was enough to still the evil of chaos, at least for a short time.

Chaos was powerful, restless; and always returned. The grandmothers had sent her, and she never forgot that.

Then came Geena and Celia. They didn't plan it that way, it just happened. The '59 Dodge Lancer—sun glinting off its fenders, with a backseat that smelled like dried herbs and stubborn memory—seemed to know the way to somewhere.

Another day, another mile. Geena sat behind the wheel of the Dodge, hands steady, her eyes scanning the coast. Celia rode beside her, as if she'd always been part of the car, her boots up on the dash, one eye scanning the horizon, the other hand resting on the hilt of a short sword.

The Dodge Lancer rumbled along the coast like a prophecy, windows down, wind braiding the two women's hair, a box of clay figures clinking gently in the trunk. They passed through woods, the scent of pine and ocean mixing like an old song. They took detours that didn't make sense.

Finally, they drove through an old, forgotten beach town just before dusk. The buildings watched them like ghosts watching from their doorways. Boards hung loose. Rusted signs swung in the breeze. Something was waiting. The old post office had a bell above it that chimed when the Dodge passed it.

No wind had touched the bell. Celia reached for her knife but stopped. Geena pressed the gas a little harder, heart pounding. The road narrowed and the pavement turned to sand and woods and sea. The Dodge Lancer, an aged warrior in its own right, kept moving forward, as if its very wheels knew the way.

Finally, they saw it. The cabin. The boat tied at the dock. Shem standing in the doorway, a beam of twilight falling across his face. They parked. No one spoke.

Marisong opened her eyes.

The old cabin stood half hidden in the dappled evening air, half-shadowed by the trees, half-lit by salt air. Ivy wound around the porch posts while the sea whispered its slow, steady hush beyond the dunes. When the rumble of the approaching car died down, Miz Wind stepped out the front door without hurry, her long braid silvering in the sun, her eyes sharp as ever. Shem stood beside her.

She studied the dusty Dodge Lancer settling into the clearing like a story finally finding its lost page. Geena climbed out first, unsure if her legs would hold. Celia followed, stretching from the long drive, her sword in its sheath tucked against her back.

Miz Wind gave a small, knowing nod.

"Come on in," she said simply, like she'd been expecting them all along. Shem nodded. The door creaked open, and the scent of lemon balm, dried herbs, and something old and comforting drifted out.

Celia glanced sideways at Geena, surprised to find her smiling like she had when Celia was a child. Something warm—something like home—wrapped around them as they crossed the threshold.

Inside, the air shifted. A kettle sang softly on the stove. The fire in the hearth was small, but warded off any chill. A cake of golden cornbread waited in a cast iron skillet. The fragrances of Goodness. The sleeping girl's presence was felt but not seen—just the faint creak of the dock in the distance, the rustle of sheets far off. Shem introduced himself.

"This is Miz Wind. People call me Shem."

He nodded at Miz Wind.

"She's been waiting for you two to get here."

"Why are we here?" Celia asked. "Or do you know?"

"Time will tell, child. For now, just rest a bit. I've got beds made up for you in the back room," Miz Wind answered.

No one said any more. They all sat down and ate hot buttered cornbread with tea and honey, then went off to sleep. There would be time for talking. For now, they were here. And they were welcome.

The '59 Dodge Lancer with fins sharp enough to cut evil things in two, stayed parked by the cabin like a watchful dog. It would play its part when the battle came—just how, none of them knew yet. But the big land yacht had always carried more than bodies. It had carried fates.

Geena had arrived hollow-eyed and weary from all her empty days, like someone who had forgotten how to dream. But as time passed, she settled into the old cabin down by the river. Her hands found clay again—cool, rich earth that remembered her touch. She began to sculpt animals and shapes that came from somewhere far deeper than memory.

She'd shaped clay before—back in the desert store days. Memories came fast and endearing. She remembered Joe Waters. Her Waterman and his blue Nash Rambler named Adam. And the three nights she'd spent with him at Washman's Draw that changed her life forever.

She wondered where he was, what ever happened to him? She dismissed Joe Waters from her mind with loving care. He'd awakened a part of her soul for her, and then headed east. It was enough. For now.

Joe Waters was a soul mate of the east. That's what he was. And always would be to her.

Shem built Geena a kiln by the sea. Each bowl, each figure, felt like a prayer fired into permanence.

Celia was different—sharp as a blade, fierce as a storm. She had learned every form of fighting—fencing, staff, swordplay—her body a moving weapon. But her mind leapt too fast. Strategy wasn't her strength.

Shem saw it. She'd need purpose, a task to channel that power. In time, though none of them knew it then, she would be sent north to help Timmon hold the north point of Light. For now, the cabin by the sea held them all—Shem, Miz Wind, Geena, Celia, and the half-awake girl with the tides in her hair.

Four women. One Walker.

The Light gathered beneath them like a deep current, slowly building complexity and Sight. Marisong was elemental, Miz Wind was wise and rooted in the old ways, Celia was youthful fire, and Geena carried grief-turned-into-hope.

Each of the four women brought something distinct to the work that lay in front of them. Power, mystery, healing, love, ancestral connection. A chorus of four women and a Walker, all unknowingly trying to anchor the eastern point of Light.

Celia practiced by kicking in boards. Geena shaped clay and wandered the land and beach. Marisong stayed awake more often now—walking among them, sitting nearby but never close enough to touch. She drifted in and out when she wanted, silent as mist.

Shem worked the place over, helping Geena place her clay figures where she said they belonged. Miz Wind watched them all, keeping a sharp eye on them. She let them know they were there for a purpose, but she didn't elaborate any further.

Only she knew that the old cabin sat dead center between the past and the future in an energy vortex that sustained the beginnings of Goodness. Atmospheric and sacred, hidden behind a mysterious, deserted, small town next to the ocean, the cabin was a stage set for an awakening, a healing or something more ominous. A battle was coming. The Earth knew. The sea knew. The mountains and forests knew. And the stars up above held their breath. And some people knew.

Then one day, at high noon—when the world held its strongest light—Miz Wind suddenly announced that it was time to see what the town held in store for them.

"I haven't been to that town in years. Something bad happened there. I don't know what. And I don't want to know."

Miz Wind shuddered.

"I drive around it to other places for the things I need."

That told them enough. Curious, they set out together to explore the abandoned town. Shem led the way. Miz Wind followed him, naming buildings in whispers. Geena touched walls with her fingertips like a sculptor sizing up raw stone. Celia shoved doors open. And Marisong, still silent, wandered just behind them, staying outside, her bare feet making no sound.

They came upon a small café that still held the scent of salt and cinnamon. A few dusty plates sat stacked on the counter. A child's shoe lay forgotten in a corner. A pair of old glasses hung from a bent nail near the window.

They didn't know it yet, but this place would matter. The deserted small town was holding its breath, waiting. Outside the café, the wind changed. It swept down from the hills like a breath held too long—dry, sour, with something strange in it. Not rot exactly, but memory.

Celia stiffened and glanced over her shoulder.

"Did you hear that?" she asked.

"No," said Shem, though his fingers tightened around the café doorframe.

Geena froze, clay-dusted hands suddenly cold. Miz Wind narrowed her eyes and stared toward the edge of the town where the asphalt cracked and weeds curled like knotted ropes.

"It's not this town," Miz Wind murmured. "It's what's underneath it."

Far below, something groaned. Not metal, not wind. Something older. The café door creaked shut behind them, though no one had touched it. Something in the town was waking up.

They ran from it, whatever it was. Back at the cabin, silence wrapped around them like a heavy blanket. No one touched their tea. Even Marisong sat still, eyes wide open now, lips pressed tight.

They didn't speak of what they'd felt in the town, but each knew now what they were up against. Something old. Twisted. Not just abandoned—but waiting.

Miz Wind lit a lantern and set it in the center of the room, its flame small but steady. "It's starting," she said softly.

That same night, a message came from the South—from the desert store's location. No one could say how, exactly. Maybe a whisper on the wind. Maybe a dream they all shared. Maybe something Miz Wind stirred from the ashes in the fireplace.

The message was clear: The dark forces had begun to move. The five points of Light—each rooted in healing chakras—were under threat. A war not of swords, but of energy and memory. And this place— this cabin and town—was one of the five.

"We gathered here for a reason," Shem said, his voice quiet. "But are we enough?" The battle for the point of Light in the East was moving toward them...

The Evil spread along the coast, rolling in like a fog no wind could lift. Drivers woke to nightmares behind the wheel, steel bending against guardrails. People in their beds thrashed under suffocating dreams. Babies cried with tiny lungs that could not draw breath. And then-just as suddenly—it passed over them.

The darkness was not here for the ordinary. They weren't wanted. It was searching for the gifted ones. For the cabin tucked near the edge of the deserted town, where an old woman kept watch and four more Light souls honed their skills. The darkness flowed toward it, deliberate and hungry, the rest of the world left behind in its choking wake.

Chapter Ten: Just Say When

Far to the north, in the wind-swept flats of Colorado, Crowell G. Restus III—still called Timmon by those who'd known him longest—stood at the edge of his land, boots planted in red dirt veined with shards of gemstones. Pine trees whispered to each other at the far boundary. The wind changed. Not far away, Manfred's Folly, Timmon's ancestral home, began growing larger and darker.

Crazy Jack had been elected mayor of Gitwell mostly because no one else wanted the job. He had taken his new position seriously, polishing the town's Welcome sign every morning with a rag that had once been his shirt.

Crazy Jack thought he had converted Gitwell to a good village, but it had started going bad again. They didn't know it all yet, not fully, but they'd felt it. He hoped he was wrong. But something was coming. That was for sure.

The metal they'd buried deep in the ground vibrated at night. Wind chimes twisted without breeze. Old dogs barked at nothing. Jack said the pine trees were nervous. Gordon thought the soil was speaking in a kind of Morse code through the maze of copper wires they had buried there.

Timmon stood still, watching the horizon. He was listening—not just with his ears, but with the fine-tuned senses passed down from his funeral-director father, and honed during his transformation into a guardian of the northern point of Light.

Then it came. A shiver through the earth. A pulse. Timmon's shoulders straightened. "It's started."

He turned and shouted, "Get ready! We build tonight!"

Thirteen miles away, Gitwell—once a ghost town, once a dark place—came alive again with movement, purpose, and sparks of Good Light in dark shadows...

Celia stood at the edge of the shore, wind blowing back her hair, the ocean reflecting flickers of starlight like scattered blades. She had slept, eaten, and stood watch. But she didn't belong in this place—not now. She could feel it.

The stillness of this place made her restless. The clay, the whispers, the sleeping woman who watched without speaking—it was all part of something deep and slow, a rhythm she admired but couldn't move to. She needed movement. She needed action. The North was calling.

Miz Wind came to her quietly. She held a small bundle wrapped in oilcloth and a red cord.

"I'll tell her. Take this with you," she said. "For sharpening and remembering."

Celia didn't ask what it meant. She tied it to her belt. Celia didn't ask for help. She *never* asked. She always just acted. Hands on hips, she glared at Geena's old '59 Dodge Lancer parked under the driftwood lean-to near the cabin. She stared at it one last time, scowling at the fact she couldn't take it.

Geena needed it—would need it—for whatever came next at the beach. The Lancer was part of

Geena, just like the clay under her fingernails these days.

Celia stormed out into the salt wind and started walking. For ten miles, she hiked the forgotten coast road, avoiding the town, sword slung across her back, boots stomping a rhythm into the earth.

And then—she spotted it. A *shimmering blue Nash Rambler,* half-buried in sea grass at the edge of a crumbling cliff. It looked wrecked. Forgotten. Covered in sea spray and old netting.

Miz Wind had once said, "What's meant for you will wait for you—unless you're a coward."

Celia wasn't a coward.

She hotwired the damn thing. It coughed to life like a stubborn dragon, belching sand and laughter. It barely had brakes, and the passenger seat was just a rusted frame—but it *moved.* And fast. So she roared west and north, hair flying, sword glinting in the rearview mirror like a warning.

She was going to Timmon, to the northern point of Light. To whatever darkness dared look her in the eye. She didn't know that the blue Nash Rambler she rode in once belonged to Geena's waterman, Joe Waters.

The road north twisted like a snake waking from sleep—narrow, cracked in places, bordered by stretches of land that looked untouched for years. The blue Nash Rambler ran better than expected, its engine humming low like a song only Geena's Joe could've taught it.

Celia drove with one hand on the wheel, the other occasionally resting on the hilt of her blade. She didn't need a map.

Something inside her—call it training, instinct, or the faint echo of Miz Wind's words—guided her towards Colorado and Crowell G. Restus III... her Timmon.

The land changed as she drove. Pine gave way to ash. Abandoned shacks stared at her with hollow windows. Fences leaned like tired men.

But then came the signs.

A rusted metal rooster, spinning in circles on a barn roof with no wind.

A dead tree weeping sap that smelled like sage.

And near the state line, a man standing on the shoulder of the highway, barefoot, wearing a blue suit three sizes too big. He saluted her and disappeared.

Celia didn't stop. She didn't speak. But her pulse picked up speed. At a gas station without a name, she filled the tank using a twenty-dollar bill from Miz Wind's coat pocket. The old woman behind the glass handed her a hard candy and whispered, "Tell the blacksmith he's almost out of time."

"I will," Celia replied, though she wasn't sure which blacksmith the woman meant.

As the Nash pushed higher into Colorado's dusty edge, the air thinned and sharpened. The world stretched wide, and the sky took on a steely hue. In the distance, low hills rolled like sleeping giants. Somewhere beyond them lay Gitwell, the little town Timmon was rebuilding with Crazy Jack, Lou, and Gordon. Celia clenched the wheel tighter. She would soon join them...

Timmon stood at the edge of his windblown land, boots rooted in dirt where sage and stone met gemstone glints. The wind blew from the south that day—sharp and dry—and it carried with it something electric. His scalp prickled. Something—or someone—was coming.

He exhaled through his nose. "Well, hell."

Behind him, Crazy Jack was arguing with Gordon about the location of the town's new forge, while Lou measured pine logs and muttered about proper beam alignment.

Timmon, or Crowell G. Restus III as his more refined instincts insisted on calling himself these days, turned slowly and looked toward the road. His eyes narrowed. He felt her. Celia. Every time she came near, the air changed. Like a magnet dragging sparks. He pulled his blacksmith apron tighter around his waist and grunted. "Keep your mind on your work, Restus," he muttered aloud. "She'll tear down a whole house if you give her half a smile."

He'd spent days hammering out iron signs, realigning quartz caches, and helping Gordon string copper threads between pine posts to catch certain frequencies of thought. They weren't sure what they were guarding against, but they all knew something was brewing. The northern point of Light had to be steady and strong.

Lou called out, "You want this cabin reinforced with stone or trust in the wind?"

Timmon wiped his hands on a rag and turned.

"Both."

Jack barked a laugh. "You hear that, Lou? The funeral man's got jokes now."

But Timmon wasn't smiling.

He'd seen something in a dream the night before. Not fire. Not flood. Fog. A heavy, crawling fog that swallowed sound and thought. And with it, the cry of a sword unsheathed, and Celia's voice, shouting his name.

"She's coming," he said softly. Lou stopped measuring. Jack looked up and laid down his hammer. Gordon nodded. They stopped work and walked away.

"Where are you going?" Timmon asked them.

"To the tool sheds," smirked Crazy Jack.

"We know where we're not wanted."

Lou gave Gordon a long stare.

"Well, Mebbe'.'"

Timmon sniffed the air. It smelled like a heat wave roaring in. Like steel shaving and carbon. Like God and Jesus and other higher powers were pushing forward. The other workers hurried away and hid.

"Yes," Timmon answered absently long after they were gone, watching the road...

The blue Nash Rambler climbed the last ridge before Gitwell and rode through town, its engine hot, windshield splattered with desert bugs. Celia gripped the wheel tighter, her jaw clenched, glancing now and then at the sword laying on the passenger seat.

"Hold together, old girl," she muttered to the car, patting the dash like it was a war horse. "We're almost there."

She studied the town. Gitwell, Colorado, looked like it had been scrubbed by wind and haunted by time.

Buildings leaned against each other like tired men after a bar fight. But there was something alive. Maybe it was new wood, new stone, or the gleaming copper laced like veins between the old buildings. The town pulsed. It breathed.

Celia frowned and slowed down. As she drove through Gitwell, figures turned toward her—workers, watchers, maybe a few ghosts. Good or bad? She didn't know.

Celia drove on out of Gitwell, the sword on the seat beside her pulsing like it had a heartbeat of its own. The blue Nash Rambler—once belonging to Joe Waters, Geena's lover, carried Geena's daughter through Gitwell like a vessel through troubled waters.

Timmon waited at the base of the Tower, hands on his hips, chin lifted as if listening to something no one else could hear. He caught her scent long before he saw her.

Metal. Road dust. That curious trace of fig bark and flame. Lavender. It wasn't just her—it was war, riding shotgun.

He watched as she brought the Nash to a sudden stop. When she jumped out of the Rambler, he said nothing. And neither did she. She ran for him, swept herself into his arms. He held her for a long minute, inhaling her scents.

"Why are you here?" he finally said.

"I had to. I'm supposed to fight here. Not on the east coast."

His eyes scanned her with affection. She waited. Finally, he nodded slowly, accepting what was. What had to be, had to be.

"It's close, then."

She gave the barest tilt of her head. "Closer than anyone knows. I was sent to stand here. I came from the point of Light in the east. Mother is there, helping to hold that point. I'm here to help hold the northern point of Light."

'Tell me more," Timmon commanded. "We've little time."

They hooked arms and walked toward the temporary bunk house he'd had erected. Timmon glanced at the Tower.

The wind shifted. "It's waking up again."

He motioned her toward the side path that led around the Tower to the stone shed he used as a war room. "You'll want to see what we've built.

And we'll need to train."

She nodded. "I came to fight."

"No doubt," he said quietly. "But I hope you came to listen, too."

Celia didn't answer right away. She laid one hand on the hilt of her sword.

"I'll listen. After I prepare."

Timmon gave her a long, unreadable look.

"We don't know exactly what we've made. Or why."

Celia followed Timmon down the narrow path. The Colorado wind was up now—sharp and circling.

They reached the shed. Inside, the war room was a patchwork of practical chaos. Maps pinned to the walls, string lines darting between thumbtacks.

Scattered notes. Chalk drawings. Piles of salvaged materials. Copper. Stone. Wire. Broken tools with meanings etched into their breaks. And in the center of it all, a huge pane of stained glass angled like a giant mirror, showing the Tower in fragments: its base, its odd jointed arms, the upper tiers—none of which seemed built with any particular purpose in mind. Celia examined the stained glass window.

"Wow. That thing," she said finally. "It's alive."

Timmon didn't blink. "That's what we think. Or maybe... aware."

"No one knows what it is?"

"Nope."

He shook his head. "The pieces of it were here before I arrived. Parts of it were scattered all over my property. Some are made of old rock. Others—newer finds—old metal of some kind. I've sent it off to be identified but haven't heard back. Then there's the carved wood. Sequoia. Petrified wood. Ancient symbols no one can read."

Celia stared. "So what is the tower for?"

"We don't know. Maybe it's a beacon. Maybe a weapon. Maybe a compass. We've all dreamed of it. Each person here has seen it in their own way. Some see it humming with light. Others, dark and pulsing. Some see birds circling the top. I saw fire once."

"And you built this whole camp around it?" she asked. Celia turned her face toward the tower. The top was shrouded in mist, though the sky remained clear.

"Does it respond to anything?" she asked.

"Sometimes," Timmon said. "We placed carved stones near it—offerings.

Certain days, they disappear. Other times, the wind picks up when someone gets too close."

"Hostile?"

"Not yet," he said. "But restless."

"Then we need to learn its moods. And fast."

Thirteen miles away, the town of Gitwell began humming like a chord tuning up for battle...

Four Points of Light were now established, each rooted in its own terrain, humming with its distinct spiritual significance.

In the **North**, Timmon's flat Colorado land held the strange and rickety stained-glass Tower, pieced together by Lou, Jack, Gordon, and Timmon. Now Celia had arrived, bringing the weight of her training and the fierce clarity of purpose that came with it.

In the **East**, Miz Wind's seaside cabin stood beside a gray, breathing ocean and a half-forgotten town. Geena, Marisong, Shem, and Miz Wind shared the space. An awakening stirred there—deep, ancient, and waiting.

In the **South**, the Desert Store pulsed steady and low. Normaine and Eddie, Emma, Avery, William, and Lily Bloome kept watch, their days spinning by like melting copper, listening to signs, waiting.

In the **West**, under the towering hush of the sequoias, Beck the Tree Whisperer and Hattie the House Whisperer tended the wounded forest, slowly coaxing life back into a land scorched and twisted by past battles.

Four Points of Light now held its Guardians. The Circle of Light was forming. Something was coming.

Chapter Eleven: The War begins

The first evidence of the evil moving toward each Point of Light came like low growls in the wind—felt more than heard.

In the **North**, the stained-glass Tower creaked in the night, its colored windows shifting without sunlight. Timmon woke to the scent of ash when there was no fire.

In the **East**, the tide pulled back too far. Birds stopped singing. Marisong woke out of a sound sleep in her boat, rowed to the dock, climbed out and went into the cabin. She woke Shem, Geena, and Miz Wind up with her first words.

"Wake up."

Miz Wind rose and hastily lit herbs of a kind that nobody had burned in decades.

In the **South**, at the Desert Store, the red wood cacti began to hum—not with rage, but with warning. Avery's Sight grew sharper. William's hands ached to hold a screwdriver and repair something, he didn't know what. Lily Jean Bloome stood over the table in the back room, drawing maps. Emma painted while Normaine hammered noisy metal chimes and Eddy made beer bread.

In the **West**, Beck heard the trees whispering in tree language. What were they saying? They stopped talking when he came near. Hattie, the gabby little House Whisperer, put them on notice.

"You better talk to Beck. Just in case you don't know what's going on here, it is serious. I know that you're older than the desert store and all the rest put together, but look what happened to you before Beck and I came here. You can't move. We can. That's a big advantage."

She huffed off. The Sequoias held a conference, using groans and spider webs and dappled sunlight to make their points. The Light glimmered and then strengthened. They would talk to Beck now. Even though he was a just a young whippersnapper of a Tree Whisperer to them.

"That's better!" Hattie exclaimed. Each Point of Light burned stronger than ever...

The mindless darkness did not care. It circled, coiled, and tested boundaries like a storm sniffing for weakness. It howled through empty places, trying to scare them off, make them flinch. But they did not flinch.

The **Central** point of Light began to stir for the first time since the evil could remember: it had only heard stories of long ago—that the darkness truly noticed. Enraged, the Evil began to move in earnest...

The spark from the **Central Point of Light** came not by chance, but because a strange gathering was moving toward it—drawn there without knowing why.

Matthew, Avery's obstinate, short-sighted, and wildly wealthy father, led the way with the confidence of a man who believed he'd already conquered every challenge worth facing. With him traveled Susan Sugar Diamond, the famous orphan-turned-author whose grit and courage had carried her through storms far darker than this.

At her side, Lana, Susan's quiet but fierce companion—now Matthew's partner, Lana was a childless earth mother in every way, strong as needed, and a caregiver.

Then there was Perry, Matthews son, who was in love with Susan Sugar Diamond. He was thoughtful, cautious, and slow to commit, but when he finally chose a course, his actions were swift and hard.

The four of them traveled west, expecting the comfort wealth gives, or at least order. Instead, the land greeted them with rusted tin cans clattering in the wind, fences sagging into the dust, and the sense of a place that had been left in disarray far too long.

Each of them—handsome, beautiful, haughty, and proud—were quietly stubborn and used to getting their own way. But the fifth Point of Light would not yield to their prideful souls. It knew more about them than they knew about themselves: both the curse and the blessing of all human beings. If the four of them were to maintain the Central Light, they would have to learn lessons.

The four of them were used to the best—good food, fine linen, soft sheets, and rooms that smelled of polish and quiet wealth. Now they were traveling in a van, chasing old, forgotten energy vortexes across back roads that barely held together. They didn't like it. Not the greasy burgers in Mom-and-Pop cafés, not the sweat-stiff clothes, not the dust that clung to everything they owned. Each stop was the same: another neglected, junky little place where the magic had long ago burned out—and then, before it could settle in their bones, they moved on again.

The dusty gravel road they traveled ended in a tangle of weeds and weathered boards at a vacant, fenced in area. Matthew got out and surveyed the place with tight-lipped disapproval. "This," he muttered, "isn't fit for a chicken to roost in."

Susan Sugar Diamond got out and ran her hand along the edge of a sun-bleached fence rail. Lana moved more slowly, squatting to touch the earth. Her fingers came away dry, dusty, and cold.

"It's not ready for us," she said quietly. "Or maybe we're not ready for it."

Perry wandered to the gate, giving it a cautious shake.

In the dusty distance stood a derelict heap of five small buildings, leaning into each other as if to keep from falling. The gate refused to open, as though the rusted hinges were locked from within.

"We're not being let in," Lana said. "Not yet. Still, it's the right place."

Reluctantly, they turned around, driving until they reached a nearby, small, half-asleep Kansas town. At the general store, they picked up camping gear—tarps, rope, a couple of mismatched lanterns—and at the edge of town, they found a low-slung motel with a buzzing neon VACANCY sign.

Over breakfast the next morning in a café that smelled of bacon and strong coffee, they asked the locals about the old place. No one gave a straight answer.

"Best leave it be," one man muttered into his plate.

"Belongs to the wind now," said a woman at the counter, her eyes narrowing.

By noon, they were back at the gate. They set up camp just outside the fence, the shadow of the buildings stretching toward them as the sun fell lower. That night, the wind rose, howling through the tin scraps, rattling cans like bones in a drum. The sound seemed to come from deep within the earth, not just the air. Shadows flickered along the fence line, dark shapes darting just outside the firelight. They could all feel it-the darkness testing them, circling, waiting for a crack.

But there was no crack. Instead, dawn arose. Dusty and morose, they ate and drank coffee. Suddenly, a gust of wind rattled the gate. The hinges groaned, and the gate swung inward. Cautiously, the four of them stepped through the open gate.

The air inside felt different—richer somehow. It was threaded with the scent of rain that hadn't fallen in years. Another gust of wind rose, swirling dust around their feet, tugging at their clothes. It circled them, then slipped its voice into their ears.

What do you want here?

The four of them froze. The wind fell into stillness. Something—unseen but present—waited for an answer. No one spoke. None of them knew. They only knew they had been drawn to this place by an urge that made no sense, yet couldn't be ignored.

Matthew, with his great physical strength and short-sightedness, Perry, with his caution and cunning, Susan, with her social adeptness, boldness, and imagination, and Lana, with her earth-mother caring and storm-proof understanding—none of them knew that they were there to become the guardians of the fifth Point of Light.

"We don't know," Matthew rumbled. They moved deeper inside the gate, boots crunching over gravel and broken glass. The buildings—five in all—leaned and sagged like weary old men. A tin roof lifted slightly in the breeze, then slapped down with a hollow bang.

"Feels like it's watching us," Lana murmured.

They reached the largest of the structures, a large, low building with no roof and a single door half-hanging from its hinges. Susan stepped inside, brushing away cobwebs as though entering an abandoned ballroom. Inside, the light was strange— thick in some corners, thin in others, as if it had been patched together from scraps.

On a far wall, a cracked mirror stood propped against empty crates. It wasn't their reflections that looked back at them. Instead, each of them saw something else—something private.

Matthew saw himself on a battlefield, swinging wildly with no aim.

Perry saw a road that split three ways, with a shadow waiting down each path.

Lana saw herself cradling a child she didn't recognize.

Susan saw a flame in her chest, flickering, almost out.

The mirror pulsed once, like a heartbeat. No one moved.

Then, from somewhere beyond the buildings, the wind rose again—low, deliberate.

Keepers are not chosen by desire, it whispered. *They are chosen by what they will give up.*

The air in the beat-up old building pressed against their chests, and they all understood—without quite knowing why—that they would not leave here the same as they arrived.

"Well, what the hell is next?" Susan muttered, folding her arms as if to keep the wind from prying inside her.

The air stilled again, so suddenly it was as if the world had taken a breath and refused to let it go. Then a sound began, soft at first, like rain against paper. It came from above the roofless house they stood in. They all looked up, mouths open in surprise.

"Not rain," Perry said in awe. "It's... seeds."

Tiny shapes swirled down from nowhere, spiraling around them, each seed glowed faintly before landing at their feet. Four kinds of seeds—different sizes, different colors.

Lana bent to pick up seeds. She cupped them in her hands. Lavender. She rolled the tiny seeds around in her palm, examining them. The tiny seeds rained around her feet, gathering close.

Matthew stared at the one huge, oval, flat shaped squash seed he held in his big, meaty hand. A few more fell around him, making spattering noises. He glanced at them knowingly. Backups. Like in a boardroom.

Perry turned the large kalonji-black cumin seeds seed over and over in his hands, searching for some kind of marking.

Susan's laughter filled the air as she grabbed a dusty tin can to gather the mix of wildflower seeds raining down around her.

Each of them quickly found something to gather their seeds in, Lana cupping hers in a folded handkerchief from her pocket, the other three using rusty tin cans.

"I guess we're supposed to plant them?" Susan asked.

No one answered. No one knew. They looked around. The earth was too dry and powdery for planting. Nothing would grow in it—not without help.

"We'll go into town," Perry decided. "Buy pots, soil... shovels... whatever... we gotta' do this right."

When they reached the gate, it slammed shut. Matthew shoved it, grunting, but it wouldn't budge. Perry searched for a latch. Lana tried speaking to the wind.

It was Susan who realized what was needed. "Set your seed cans down. They have to stay here. Inside."

They set the cans down. Matthew's heavy squash seeds. Lana's lavender drifted like perfume in the air. Perry's black cumin seeds coiled into little piles. Susan shook her can until the wildflower seeds rattled like dry, whispering, dancing rain.

The gate swung open as if nothing had ever barred their way.

They didn't talk much on the drive into town— just the low hum of the tires on the dirt road and the occasional sigh when someone's thoughts got too loud to hold in.

At the hardware store, Matthew hauled bags of rich potting soil onto the cart like he was stacking firewood for the longest winter anyone could encounter. Perry picked out terracotta pots, checking each one for cracks. Lana found a watering can shaped like a goose and added it to the pile. Susan wandered between aisles, tossing in gloves, twine, and, at the last minute, a little bell she claimed would "keep the energy moving."

They stopped at the small grocery next door to the garden center and loaded up on bread, cheese, tins of beans, and enough coffee to keep Matthew civil. The shopkeeper eyed their pile of soil and pots but didn't ask questions. In small towns that resided next to many odd unknowns, people knew better.

By afternoon, they were back at the gate. It stood open this time, waiting. They carried everything in, the wind curling through their hair and down their collars and left the gardening things in the roofless house.

For a moment, each of them felt the brief taste of Goodness, but it was gone before they could catch hold of it.

The old house smelled of rust and dust but underlying it was something more—green things trying to grow in the dark. Each of them felt it, though none spoke it aloud: these seeds were not ordinary.

Later in time, they would learn that each seed was a weapon of its own—an unseen root, a hidden bloom, a scent or shape or strength that could break the enemy in ways steel or guns and knives never could. But that night, they only knew to keep the seeds safe behind the gate that seemed to guard them as much as keep others out...

The next day, they began to plant. The area inside the roofless house slowly took shape—rows of pots lined up against walls, soil dark against the pale boards. Between trips to town for food, tools, and clothes, they worked.

"This camping's fine for now," Perry said, setting down a sack of nails, "but we can't do this forever. We need to live better."

It was during one of those trips that Matthew called the Desert Store. He'd meant only to check on supplies—but the voice on the other end stopped him cold. Avery was alive!

For a moment, Matthew couldn't breathe. The world narrowed to the crackling phone line, the faint background hum of the store. He didn't speak. Didn't move.

By the time he hung up, his face was ashen. Perry caught him before he could fall. They drove him straight to the small-town hospital, the old truck rattling on the uneven road.

Perry stayed with him through the night. In the morning, they returned to the gate, the others waiting. The seeds had been watered. They were growing much quicker than expected. Almost overnight, they had rushed into life as if being fed an invisible fertilizer.

The campfire burned low. The air inside the fence felt heavier now—expectant, as if it, too, had heard the news.

Perry drove back to town and called Avery from the pay phone.

"Where are you?" Avery asked.

"In Kansas. Out by a little town named Body. On some land the four of us have been... called on to "improve" for some reason or another. Everybody's healthy. We're okay."

Avery's voice sharpened. "Tell Matthew to face me—in the New Mexico direction. And apologize. At six p.m. just before dusk. Do it tomorrow night. I'll be facing him back."

Perry blinked. "Will do. What the hell are we doing here? Do you know, Avery?"

Avery hesitated, then said, "Stay there, brother. It's serious."

Something in his voice was different. Avery laid it out for Perry. When he finished, he said, "Maybe you're to hold the Fifth point of Light. Maybe you four have been called to hold the center," Avery said thoughtfully. "No one knows just how this works. We just do what comes to us."

"It's just people that had something to do with the desert store that are called to do this... whatever it is?"

"Looks that way. Although others do drop by and help sometimes. They usually bring a skill we don't have. Something is coming—something evil."

"You know we're too damn old to be doing this crap, don't you?"

"Yep. Tell that bastard father of yours to call."

"I love you, brother," Perry said in a low voice. "Thank God you're back."

Perry hung up and drove back through the Kansas dust to the small cluster of abandoned buildings. He found Matthew pacing near the gate and delivered Avery's message flatly.

Matthew erupted—shouting, fists clenched. "I hate myself! Isn't that enough?" he bellowed.

"You should be glad he's even willing to talk to you," Perry shot back.

"I want to go to him—I'm leaving right now! Phone isn't good enough!"

"We all have to stay here. Can't you tell, you big lummox, that something's going on? That we're preparing for some kind of psychic war or battle again? Like we fought at the store" Lana scolded. She stepped in close, her voice firm but calm, putting a hand on his shoulder, guiding him away from the others.

Matthew let Lana steer him toward the campfire. The flames crackled, snapping bits of dry grass into the air. He dropped heavily onto a folding chair, shoulders slumped, staring into the fire as though it had answers.

Nobody spoke for a while. Even the wind had quieted, as if waiting for the next move.

Then—faint, so faint they almost missed it—the earth gave a low hum. It came up through their boots, into their bones, a steady thrum like the heartbeat of something buried deep.

Lana straightened. "Did you feel that?"

Susan nodded, eyes narrowing toward the dark silhouette of the old buildings. "It knows we're here."

Perry tossed another stick into the fire. "It knows and doesn't like it one bit."

Somewhere beyond the fence, a can rattled. The wind picked up again—whispering, circling—before falling into stillness.

By morning, the seeds had more than sprouted. Not all at once—some were just green slivers pushing through the soil in the dusty pots, others were already lifting broad leaves toward the sunlight as if they'd been waiting for centuries for the patch of sun coming through the roofless house.

Lana's lavender, almost full grown, shimmered faintly, a pale silver mist curling off the leaves when the wind passed through the door. Matthew's full grown squash plant had a stubborn set to its thick stem, already twisting towards the gate like it meant business. Perry's black cumin sprouted spiky, feathery green stems towards the sky, flowering, its shadow looking far larger than it should. Susan's wildflowers spilled over their tin cans, riotous, tangling, rooting into the dusty ground with abandon, reaching toward anything that moved. The plants were beautiful and alive in a way that made the air hum.

Matthew drove into Body the next morning. He jumped out and strode to the pay phone. He fed coins into the pay phone, dialed the number on the scrap of paper he carried, and gripped the receiver like it might run away.

The phone rang forever before Avery picked up.

"Matthew." Avery's voice was flat, businesslike. No hint of anything Matthew could read. He didn't know what to say.

Finally he said, "I'm in Kansas at that land Perry told you about. Figured I'd—"

Avery cut in. "Where's those bitches you traded me for?"

Matthew's jaw clenched. "They're alive. In France. I keep them there. Hemmed in. I could have ruined them when I found out you didn't do it, but I keep them where I can watch them."

Matthew's throat worked, the words came slow.

"I didn't believe them. Not all the way. But I didn't fight for you either. I should have. And I can't fix that. I can only tell you I'm here now. I'll stand where you tell me to stand."

Silence hummed between them. Then Avery said, almost grudgingly, "This isn't about us. Something's coming. Something worse than what they did. You want to redeem yourself? Stay where you're at and do your job for once without bitching or going off half cocked. I don't want to see you, and don't like that you're a part of this."

Matthew shut his eyes. "Avery..."

"You will have to face in the direction of the desert store at six each evening. I will face Body, Kansas. You. That will strengthen the lines of Light between us. I hope I don't have to do it very long."

"Ok, son. I'll do whatever you say."

"Don't call me son. Call me Avery."

The line went dead.

Matthew stood in the dusty Kansas street, the pay phone cooling in his hand, remembering the little boy who'd once looked up at him like he could fix anything. The boy he'd failed. The boy who'd turned into a man who didn't trust him. Somewhere deep in Matthew's chest, a weight shifted—just enough to hurt worse than before.

That evening, he went out to the open field just inside the gate.

The sky was turning rust at the edges. West—that's where Avery would be looking from New Mexico. The wind moved slow. He could hear the grass scrape together. A hawk circled once, far off, like it was keeping an eye on him.

"I'm here," he said. The words felt strange in his mouth.

The ground gave a faint thump under his boots. Not much. Just enough to know Avery had heard, in whatever way this worked. It wasn't forgiveness. Wasn't even close.

A smell came on the wind—mesquite and smoke.

Matthew stood there until the light left. He knew Avery was doing the same on his end. Neither of them crossed the distance. Neither of them turned away...

Chapter Twelve: The Delve Into Power

By the third morning, they'd stopped treating the plants like they were just plants. Lana knelt by her lavender every sunrise, brushing the soft leaves with her fingertips. A scent arose, not just sweet but piercing, cutting through weariness and irritation, leaving her mind clear. When the others breathed the scent in, they felt the same clarity. The lavender could *calm storms in the head*—the kind that cloud judgment or make hands shake.

Matthew's squash had doubled in size overnight, its vines thick as rope. When he touched one, it moved—wrapping gently around his wrist before uncoiling. He grinned like a boy with a new tool. "Defense," he said. "Strong enough to stop whatever pushes through that gate." The vines seemed to agree, inching toward the fence as though patrolling.

Perry's black cumin stayed low, unassuming, until he crushed a single seed between his fingers. The scent that burst out was sharp, biting, almost metallic. When he scattered a few seeds along the ground, ants and beetles that had been chewing at the squash turned back as if struck. He didn't say it out loud, but he knew the cumin was for *driving things away.*

Susan's wildflowers were chaos—every color, every shape, blooming all at once. But she noticed something: where her flowers leaned, light followed. Even the shadows seemed thinner around them. She began placing pots near the darker corners of the yard, and by nightfall, those spots felt warmer, safer.

"They spread light," she told the others. "They'll find the holes and fill them."

They worked in quiet cooperation after that. Lana's lavender for focus. Matthew's squash for defense. Perry's cumin for repelling. Susan's wildflowers for illumination.

The plants responded more when they were tended—almost eager. And when the darkness outside circled the gate that night, it found a fence lined with leaves and petals that hummed with stubborn, living light.

Along with working the plants in the roofless house, they spent hours on the place next door— what passed for their future shelter. The motel's thin mattresses and buzzing neon were already behind them. No more white linen lines or soft pillows. Those days were gone, packed away with everything else that used to mean comfort.

They couldn't bring in anybody to do the work for them. The gate had slammed shut the first time they tried that. Now it was brooms and buckets, hammer and nails, and trips to town for water and whatever Body's little hardware shop or junk piles could offer. They swept dust into the wind until it choked them, pried loose boards that clung like stubborn teeth, and patched holes with whatever fit.

The walls became a strange patchwork—slats of dented tin roofing, old black school slates with faint chalk ghosts still on them, marbled sheets of copper flashing that caught the light in sharp streaks. It was odd. Weird. And somehow, it worked. They followed their instincts while building.

People from the edge of town began to notice. A rancher dropped off a load of wood "no use to him." Someone else brought nails. A woman in a long denim coat leaned on the gate one afternoon, offering to sell them three narrow beds, the springs intact, the frames rust-free.

"You'll need 'em," she said. "Whatever's coming, you won't fight it well on the floor."

They didn't ask how she knew. They took her up on her offer and asked for a fourth bed.

It wasn't long before they noticed that the plants in the roofless house seemed to stand taller, their leaves angling toward the glow of reflected light off the copper sheeting they'd placed here and there on the walls.

Lana's lavender gave off a sharper scent, rolling in low waves that calmed even Matthew when his temper rose. Perry's black cumin seeds, still small and stubborn, pushed up in tight rows as if laying claim to their ground. Susan's wildflowers began showing green faster than any of them expected, their scattered placement forming patterns she swore she hadn't planned. And Matthew's squash plant, broad and steady, seemed to tilt toward the patched walls, as if guarding them.

At night, when the copper caught the moonlight, the air inside the building shifted—warmer, almost charged. A faint hum ran through the floorboards, and, more than once, Perry swore the tin walls gave off a low ring, like a struck bell.

"Old junk singing to us," Susan muttered, though she didn't sound entirely joking.

They didn't know it yet, but every strike of the hammer, every strange scrap of metal they wedged into place, was weaving the shelter into the same unseen current the plants had tapped into. Copper pulling energy, tin carrying it, slate holding it still. Together, the plants and the patched walls were shaping something—something growing, something meant to hold onto Goodness at any cost when the time came.

Everyone, plants and people, kept preparing. It was only a matter of time before whatever was coming would test them all...

Avery was angry. Everything he was doing had to wait. He would have to visit the red cactus desert again, take the edge off before he said or did something he couldn't undo. That place knew how to strip a man down and set him back on his feet.

How much more was he supposed to lose?

Matthew—his father—gone to him long ago in every way that counted. Mama, his innocent sweetheart, the only woman who ever made the world feel steady, was buried faraway in Spain. His mother—blood and nothing else—had ditched him and Perry for some duke in Europe and locked the door behind her. Wouldn't see them. Wouldn't even send a note.

So many losses, and now the air smelled like more was coming. Worse than before. He wanted revenge, real bad. He ached and burned with revenge. But not a sloppy kind of revenge. The real slow kind. The kind that makes sure the ones who deserved it knew exactly who it came from.

But first, the red cacti.

The red cacti stood waiting to take his rage, their silence deep enough to let him hear himself again. Out there, he could let the fury burn through, leave it under the open sky, and come back the man everyone counted on—the steady, staid one who could stand at the center of the storm and point the way when the nightmare show started.

And it was coming.

Avery left the red cactus desert standing happily with fresh red paint. The rusty cans at their base rattled in the wind, a dry, hollow sound thanking him. The sound followed him back to the truck. When he reached the desert store, the sun was still high.

William was out front, leaning against the rail, hat low over his eyes. Lily Jean Bloome sat on the porch steps, peeling an orange slow, like she was timing each curl of rind.

Avery stepped out of the truck, slammed the door. The red dust still clung to him, his knuckles raw, a streak of sweat dried down his cheek. He moved lighter, though—like something had been unhooked from his shoulders.

William tipped his hat back, eyes following him to the front door. "You go out to the cacti again?"

Avery didn't stop. "Yep."

Inside, the air felt cooler, shaded by the old shelves and worn counters. The store smelled of coffee and dust, a grounding sort of scent. Avery poured himself a mug, took a slow sip, and stared out the front window where the sunlight bent in.

He knew that something had to be healed between him and his father. Facing each other from a distance every day until that happened. He didn't like it. And he suspected Matthew didn't either. A small curl of amusement ran through him. Maybe they were both in the same boat. Crap!

William and Lily Jean Bloome stayed quiet, reading him the way they always did—by what he didn't say. They didn't need to hear the words to know he could hold steady now for whatever came next...

The five points of Light were becoming stronger each day. Each one feeding the others like they'd been waiting for this moment their whole lives.

The enemy knew it, too. Knew that if they let the beams grow much more, they'd be too strong to crack. So they attacked early.

The attack started small, subtle—just a shift in the air, a thickness that made the back of the neck prickle. Then the shadows leaned in closer than they should, sliding over ground they'd never touched before. Windows rattled in places no wind had reached. Dogs in three different towns went silent all at once.

Evil made its move.

Not all at once, but in thin, needling pushes meant to find the weak spots. And somewhere between the red cactus desert and the center in Kansas, the first strike hit.

It came in like a sickness. Not the kind that knocked you flat, but the kind that sat behind your eyes and whispered you'd never be well again.

The red cactus desert felt it first. The air shifted—just enough to make them creak in their rusty cans. The sound carried wrong, bent sideways. The heat was the same, but it sat heavier, like it was watching them.

In Kansas, Matthew woke with his fists clenched around nothing. Perry's coffee turned bitter halfway through a sip, though the pot was fresh. Lana looked up from her lavender seedlings and swore the color had dulled. Susan, who had never been afraid of anything, found herself turning around three times before walking out of the roofless house.

Out west, in the Sequoia clearing, Beck stopped mid-swing with an axe. No wind, no sound—just a stillness that set every nerve on edge.

And at the seaside cabin in the east, Miz Wind went to the shore and stood for a long time, watching the horizon where the sky was too dark for morning.

Evil had made its first touch. Not to destroy— yet—but to mark them. To let them know it was coming and it knew where they were.

A short time later, evil struck again. The wind over the Kansas point of Light shifted, carrying the faintest whiff of rot. It slid through the fence slats, testing the air, curling around the buildings like a thief's hand.

Matthew was first to feel it. His squash vine, thick as a wrestler's arm, rattled in its bed of dirt. The leaves hardened, edges serrated like old saw blades. A sound started low in the vine—something between a growl and the crack of wood splitting. Matthew didn't understand it all yet, but he knew this: the plant could *cut*—and anything that brushed those leaves without permission would bleed.

Perry's black cumin plants stiffened, their pods turning inward, storing heat until they trembled. When he brushed one, it snapped open with a sting, shooting fine black shards into the air. They hung there, waiting. Perry grinned a little. "Shrapnel," he muttered. "Good."

Lana's lavender swayed though there was no wind. The scent thickened, not sweet now, but sharp, invasive, forcing the rot-smell back. She realized it could flood a whole space with calm that wasn't kindness—it was control, slowing everything it touched, holding it in place long enough for the others to strike.

Susan's wildflowers glimmered faintly at the edges, their colors too bright in the dull afternoon. One petal fell. When it touched the dust, it hissed, and a black tendril of whatever was trying to seep in shriveled away. She crouched down, plucking a handful of petals, tucking them into her pockets. "Never know when you'll need a weapon you can hide in plain sight," she said to nobody in particular.

Above them, the light beaming from the Kansas point held steady—but now it had teeth. Four plants. Four groups. Four directions. Four other points of Light. Waiting.

All five Points of Light now had its own group of keepers, skills, and tools. Each could work on their own, but got a boost when linked together.

In Colorado, (North Point) Timmon's tower and stained glass could bend and focus Light into different frequencies.

On the east coast (East Point) in Carolina, Marisong, Miz Wind, and Shem were working with the water and wind forces. East could carry those forces over vast distances to drown/dilute the enemy's hold.

At the Desert Store in New Mexico, (South Point) Avery Mott Judson, William the Dude, Lily Jean Bloome, Normaine and Eddy, and Emma stood ready to defend the grounding forces that stabilized the five Points of Light.

At the Sequoia Clearing (Western Point) in northern California, Hattie the House Whisperer, and Beck the Tree Whisperer, most of the healing of the trees from the last attack was done. Now they were ready.

At the fifth Point of Light, Matthew's squash plant had become a "slicing frequency" sent to the other points of Light. In Colorado, Timmon noticed a new razor-edge beam slicing a shadow before it hit the tower.

Perry's black cumin shrapnel turned into airborne particles that blended with Miz Wind's gales, shredding the darkness midair before it could root.

Lana's lavender slowed the enemy's advance so the red desert cacti and the desert store could hit back with maximum force.

Wind carried Susan's wildflower acid-petals west to Hattie and Beck, to drip into the soil and dissolve the enemy's corruption so regeneration could start instantly.

Matthew's squash vine had thickened, each broad leaf edged like a blade. When the wind passed through, the edges hissed as if testing a cut.

Perry's black cumin stalks had grown dense and dark, seed pods rattling like dry bones in a tin can. One pod split as Perry touched it, releasing a faint peppery grit into the wind that made him cough. On the coast, that grit in the wind caught a creeping darkness and shredded it into nothing.

Lana's lavender stood in neat clusters, purple spikes swaying even when there was no wind, the scent so sharp it seemed to slow time for a second. At the desert store, the red wooden cacti flared hotter, their energy burning clean and fast, the heat pulling the anger out of the Shadows standing near them.

Susan's wildflowers were a riot of colors that didn't belong in this place—yellow, crimson, blue so deep it felt like looking into water. Their petals dripped sticky dew that smoked on the dusty floor and cleansed anything below it of evil. In the west, Hattie and Beck watched blackened soil fizzle and turn green, the change moving quicker than they'd ever seen.

Back in Kansas, none of them knew. They only saw their plants in the pale morning light, felt the faint hum in the air, and thought maybe—just maybe—they were doing something right.

That night, the wind came from the wrong direction. Cold, crawling. It slid through the fence, slipped between the slats of the half-built walls, and carried with it a smell like damp ashes.

They were sitting by the fire, eating canned beans, when Matthew's squash vine began thrashing. It had overgrown its pot long ago and now was rooted all along the wall. Its leaves slapped the air like something unseen was moving through them. The backup seeds had grown and spilled along behind it. They writhed, looking for something to dissect. Perry's cumin stalks rattled hard enough to spill seeds on the dusty floor.

"Earthquake?" Susan asked, looking around.

Lana shook her head. "No. It's them."

The air thickened, as if the night itself were leaning in. A shadow skittered along the fence line, low and quick. Another darted behind the derelict shed.

The squash vine whipped forward—one leaf slicing the air. A long, wet *rip* sounded, and a hunched shape detached from the darkness, screaming like it had been burned. It crumpled into black dust.

Perry's cumin pods burst all at once, a peppery haze exploding into the wind. The shapes stumbled, gagging, their outlines blurring as if they couldn't keep themselves together.

The lavender flared—color brighter than any moonlight—its scent shooting outward in an invisible wave. The shapes staggered back, claws curling inward.

Then Susan's wildflowers leaned toward the fence. Their sticky dew flung itself into the dark, splattering over one shadow. The thing gave a sound like a sack of glass breaking and then nothing.

The wind shifted, pulling the ashes away. The Shadows were gone.

They stared at the plants. The plants stood still again, leaves glistening faintly.

"Guess we know what they're for now," Perry muttered.

But what none of them saw—what no one here would know until much later—was that in Colorado, the tower lights had burned brighter for a full minute. On the coast, the sea glowed gold for a breath. In the west, the forest's new green spread in a perfect ring. And at the desert store, Avery felt the red cacti hum from a distance. The fifth Point of Light had answered. And the others had heard.

The evil ones scoffed at the idea of plants besting them. Green things were beneath notice—fragile, breakable, a meal for fire. They had only prepared for ruin, for destruction, not for life itself rising against them. But the Earth knew. The Earth always knew. Its business was not rage or conquest—it was renewal. Roots wrapped around shadows, blossoms opened against smoke, and leaves whispered truths the dark could not unhear. What the enemy dismissed had become the weapon they could not overcome...

Chapter Thirteen: Fighting Evil

The Earth took war zones back, as it always has. Paved streets buckled and crumbled, their neat lines breaking under the pressure of roots. Houses sagged, beams splitting, roofs bowing to vines that pushed through shattered windows. What wars left behind—poisons, smoke, ash—the Earth sent wild green things to answer. Wild shoots sprouted where blood had spilled. Tough weeds drank up toxins. Flowers no one had planted opened along the ruins, each bloom a quiet act of defiance. The evil ones hadn't understood. They only knew how to destroy. The earth knew how to renew.

By the next night, the Kansas air was wrong again—thicker, heavier, like it had been wrung out and left to rot. Even the stars looked dim.

They were inside the roofless house, oil lamps throwing weak halos over the pots, when the wind hit—no warning, no build-up, just a blast that shoved against the walls, bringing with it a sound like metal dragging over stone.

The lavender shivered first, bowing low. The squash leaves curled inward, like armor plates locking down. The cumin bent, seeding itself in a burst of tiny black sparks. Susan's wildflowers opened wide—too wide—petals spreading into something sharper.

Lana's voice was low, but steady. "They're coming for us."

The shadows didn't creep this time. they poured over the fence like a flood. Dozens, maybe more. Too many to count, shapes bending and twitching, sometimes human, sometimes not. Their eyes weren't eyes at all, but pits of pale light.

Matthew grabbed the broken hoe they'd been using to till the dirt. Perry found himself with a hammer in hand. It wouldn't be enough—not against this.

The plants moved first. Lavender threw its light in a blinding wave, turning the front line of shapes into silhouettes that tore apart mid-stride.

The squash vine lashed out in thick whips, each strike landing with the weight of a sledgehammer. The ground shook where it hit. The cumin burst again, but hotter this time, the air filling with a choking, burning spice that made the things stumble and shriek.

The wildflowers spit a sticky red sap that hissed when it touched shadow-flesh, eating through it like acid.

They fought in rhythm without speaking. Matthew smashed whatever the vine knocked down. Perry drove his hammer into anything that got through the spice haze. Lana stayed near the lavender, pushing its blooms toward the thickest dark. Susan kicked over a half-empty bucket, letting the sap spread in a slick barrier.

For the first time, the shadows fell back, not vanishing, but regrouping. The wind carried their whispers over the fence: *We'll cut you from the root.*

The four of them stood there in the shaking glow of their plants, breathing hard, listening to the night go still.

Somewhere far away, in the desert store, Avery's hand clenched around his favorite coffee cup.

In the tower in Colorado, the light wavered, then steadied. On the coast, the waves drew back farther than they should, as if waiting. In the west, a hush fell over the trees. The war had officially begun. Kansas was now a target.

It didn't take long for the next strike. By the second night, the beams were pulsing—steady, solid, almost taunting the dark. That's when it happened.

First, a low hum, like something chewing through the ground. Then the wind shifted—not in Kansas, but from Kansas. It was being pulled, dragged east.

Matthew straightened. "They're splitting the attack."

William's voice crackled through the radio Avery had sent them: *Coast's under it. Miz Wind says they're crawling out of the surf like they own the place. You've got to send what you can. Now.*

"How the hell do we send anything?" Perry snapped.

The answer came from the plants. The lavender's glow brightened to a near-piercing white. A tendril of it pulled upward, bending east like it could smell the ocean. The squash vine coiled, then anchored itself deep into the floor, feeding its strength into the lavender's light. The cumin split into seed, spinning fast enough to make the air burn. The smoke rose, curling into the light-stream.

The wildflowers bled sap into a clay pot Susan shoved under the lavender's stalk. The Light drank it in, turning sharp and focused. The light beam shot east like a laser—through the wall, over the fence, beyond Kansas.

On the coast, Miz Wind watched the light beam hit the beach like a spear. Sea-slick shadows froze mid-charge, their forms hardening, brittle. Marisong's wave took them apart in one clean sweep.

But the enemy wasn't giving up in Kansas. While half the plant-power poured into the beam, the rest of the garden tightened its defenses. Vines moved like guards, cumin smoke thickened, lavender pulsed to keep the fence line clear.

William's voice came again, sharper this time: *It worked. But they'll try this again. They know we can link now. Don't let 'em cut the line.*

The wind died down. For a moment it was so quiet they could hear the seeds still ticking in the cumin pods.

Perry exhaled. "Well... now we know we're not just farming."

No one laughed.

The evil hit again just after dawn. No warning this time—just the sharp *snap* of something breaking in the air, like a wire pulled too tight.

In Kansas, the lavender shot upright, leaves quivering. The squash vines twisted in sudden agitation, their flat seeds vibrating inside the pods. Perry swore under his breath. "They're here."

At the same moment, near the desert store, the six red wood cacti leaned toward the west as if listening.

Avery set his coffee cup down with a thud. It was his first cup of the day.

"They're going for the trees."

In the Sequoia grove, Beck felt it first. The ground shivered, just enough to make the pine needles whisper. Then came the smell—hot, metallic—like something trying to scorch the roots from the inside out.

Hattie pressed her palm to the nearest trunk. "They're trying to cook 'em alive!"

Kansas attacked back. Lana's lavender shot a beam south-west, splintering halfway into two beams of Light—one going toward the desert store, one going toward the west coast Sequoias.

Perry had had enough. Slow to boil and slow to decide, he didn't hesitate.

The black cumin joined in, sending sharp shards of smoke with the light, changing it from gold to a deep burnished red.

The squash didn't beam. Instead, it pushed its roots so far down that the ground in Kansas trembled, sending a deep *thump* westward—carrying power to the desert floor.

The red wood cacti absorbed the thump like a heartbeat, their rusty milk cans rattling until they spat out sparks. Cowboy Johnson grabbed a handful of the glowing shavings and hurled them into the desert wind. They turned into whirling, red-hot slivers that raced back towards the Sequoia grove.

In the grove, the trees took it in, their sap running hotter, their roots glowing faint orange. The earth around the Sequoias stopped trembling, the heat from the enemy cut in half.

But Kansas wasn't so lucky. The Shadows had learned—this time they came in silence, low to the ground, avoiding the light until they were almost under it. One leapt the fence, teeth bared.

Matthew was on it before it landed. He slammed it with a length of rusted copper from the roofless house wall. The thing screamed—not like an animal, but like something burning—and crumbled into black grit. Three more took its place.

From the west, Hattie's voice came through the link—thin, ghostlike, but clear: *Hold 'em, old shanties in Kansas. Help our people. Ten more breaths.*

Lavender flared, wildflowers bled more sap, the cumin smoke thickened until it was almost solid. The squash vine whipped out like a rope, catching another shadow mid-leap and crushing it into the dirt.

On the eleventh breath, the light from Kansas and the west collided overhead, bursting into a shockwave. The Shadows dissolved. Sweet, clean wind returned.

Perry sniffed the air gratefully. He leaned on his knees, gasping. "That was... both of us at once!"

Matthew straightened slowly. "Yeah! And next time, I'm guessing it'll be worse. Damn! I wish I wasn't so old!"

He grinned. "Well, at least I've still got plenty of muscle...here and in the boardroom!"

In Colorado, Timmon and his crew were on high alert. Something was wrong nearby—close enough that the air over the flat land felt cold and heavy, as if the ground itself was holding its breath.

It began with a low hum coming from inside the Folly, the ugly, hulking structure down the road from where they had built the tower.

Until recently, Timmon hadn't known the Folly existed. It was a sprawling, dark, ugly, misshapen thing, part evil mansion, part evil ruin. The Folly had been the last sanctuary of Vance Swain, an evil man, and hateful, evil Mina, Timmon's mother. They had died there a short time ago. Timmon had thought his ordeal with his mother's evil was over, that the Folly was weakened and going down now. It was a house that could never be lived in, but it could stay as he had left it. But he was wrong. He had underestimated the evil dwelling there.

He didn't know that the Folly sat dead center on its own negative energy chakra, which had influenced his Good ancestors into becoming evil.

Mina and Vance's deaths had stirred the dark forces in that energy vortex into action. The Folly joined bigger forces that did not intend to lose the Folly. Or Body, Kansas. Or Gitwell, Colorado. Or the small town of Binder near the Sequoias in northern California.

Timmon stood in the tower's doorway, studying the black shape on the horizon. The Folly wasn't just humming now—it was breathing, inhaling the cold air in long, greedy gulps.

"Time to end it," Timmon said.

Celia clasped his hand. "Then let's do it fast!"

They sent Crazy Jack into Gitwell to keep an eye on things there, for the Folly had once been Gitwell's deepest root.

Gordon and Lou stayed on the outskirts of the rampage, tossing things out of the way and magicing what needed it.

Timmon and Celia moved fast. They ran into the evil old house. Using just the tools they trusted—iron bars, hammers, sledgehammers, knives, and screwdrivers, they began tearing the place down.

The Folly fought back. Doors slammed before they could be opened. Windows hissed with a wind that tried to burn their skin. The floor pitched under their boots, trying to throw them down the crooked stairwells. In the upstairs hallway, the wallpaper began to bleed.

Vance's voice—thin, mocking—slid along the walls. Mina's voice followed, sharper, digging in where it knew it could hurt. Hate dripped from every word they spoke, every corner, like a slow green poison. Their words weren't meant to scare them. They were meant to keep them there, in the house's grip, long enough for something worse to arrive.

But Timmon and Celia didn't stop.

Suddenly a bell-shattering noise rolled down from the tower, obliterating the hiss and spit of hate, replacing it with the clean, ringing noises of Hope. The Folly began to shake.

Timmon remembered. Noise, sound, vibration—these could take down a monastery in Tibet. Why not this edifice of evil?

As the house shook and fell apart, Timmon and Celia tore through the Folly's rotten belly, prying loose what they could and hurling the foul, falling debris out to Gordon and Lou, who chanted over each twisted scrap, burning away its venom with spellfire.

The Tower bells rang harder. The Folly screamed a long, tearing wail that rose until it split, splintered, and died in the sound of a thousand boards giving way. When the dust cleared, the hulking shape was gone. Only an ugly heap of broken beams, warped metal, slick ropes of slime, and black smoke remained. The hum was gone. The breathing, gone.

The Tower stopped ringing.

Crazy Jack drove up, stayed out in the road, rolled down his window, and shouted, "Everything's okay in town!"

Timmon didn't answer right away. His eyes were fixed on the wreckage—the heap of blackened beams, splintered boards, twisted metal. "One less place for them to hide," he said, heartbreak in his voice. The ruins had been more than just The Folly to him. They were the last remnants of his mother's bloodline. The women before her—his grandmothers, had walked those halls. Their shadows still hung in the air. Crazy and wanting. Never learning better. He hoped there might have been one good soul among them, just one he could claim with pride. Now, he would never know.

The thought pierced him harder than the fight had. The rubble was final. The past was sealed.

"Burn it all. Let's have an end to this... horror," Timmon said coldly. Lou and Gordon began burning what was left of the Folly.

Chapter Fourteen: The Battle Ends

Timmon wondered—not for the first time—why he was to lead this battle for Good, when he came from an evil mother. Well, he was Crowell Goforth Restus the Third. He had chosen his father's path.

He straightened his shoulders and turned back to the Tower. Celia wrapped her arms around him like she could shield him against his hurt.

Lou nodded as Gordon said, "You go on. You've done enough. We'll see to the rest."

The wind shifted sharply. A deep, rolling vibration came across the plains—too steady for thunder, too heavy for anything harmless. The enemy had felt the blow. Timmon's eyes hardened, though the sorrow never left them.

"They'll be back," he said flatly, "And we'll be ready."...

Crowell Goforth Restus the Second—Undertaker from another world, father to Timmon—waited until Timmon and Celia left before he began The Folly's funeral rites. They didn't know that the black mind beneath the rubble still lingered, that it would rise again unless it was bound to the grave it deserved. There was no goodness in the burning boards, no Light in the black ashes—only venom waiting to crawl back. Crowell opened his case of ancient tools, whispered the words that bent time and silence, and set to work. This wasn't burial. It was exile.

And when the last chant faded, the Folly was gone—not destroyed, but banished, gnawing at itself in the Otherworld, far from the living.

Crowell Goforth Restus the Second—Undertaker from another world, father to Timmon—moved like a shadow behind the Guardians who held the five Points of light. He never stayed long, never interfered openly. His place was at the edges of things, tending to matters only someone in his Undertaker position could understand.

It was Crowell who bound the Folly's mind so it couldn't rise again. It was Crowell who turned aside things too twisted for the innocent Guardians to face directly.

He watched his beloved son Timmon with quiet, constant vigilance—not guiding, not intruding, simply protecting, ensuring his son could walk his path without stumbling into traps older than the war itself.

No one spoke of him. Few even noticed him. But without him, whole battles would have been lost before they began...

The next attack began like a single note struck in the dark — deep, slow, and endless. Everyone felt the change, knew the bad stuff was coming again. From the Sequoias in the West, to the Tower in Colorado, to the shacky cabin by the eastern sea, to the desert store on its sunburnt chakra, the enemy attacked them all at once.

The West Point -The Sequoias

The evil moved west from Kansas in the next few hours. Far from Colorado, in the western clearing where the great Sequoias towered, the air shifted. The ancient trees—older than dynasties, older than the enemy's first breath—began to stir in their roots. Their branches whispered not in the wind, but in their wisdom.

They would fight this battle in their own way—using the *weight of knowing*. They had been seedlings and grown into towering trees before the first evil arrived on these shores. They had survived many dull and stupid wars—they planned to survive this one. But they were trees. They couldn't move. Only Beck the Tree Whisperer held the power to direct them.

Beck watched the Sequoias needles tremble, releasing a rain made of Light unlike sunlight: golden, warm, and heavy with the wisdom of the ages. That Light fell over the battlefield like a slow, deliberate blessing. The enemy flinched under it, for evil cannot stand to be *seen* in the pure light of truth.

But such a rain also made the Sequoias targets. The enemy would try to fell them—if they could. Hattie knew the trees gift came at a price. Each drop of golden rain cost the Sequoias a piece of themselves. Beck knew it too, though he said nothing. It was the way it was.

Hattie had made the Clearing into a home. The Sequoias lined the clearing like protective walls. Hattie and Beck became the trees' shields.

Beck fought at the edges, his axe and longbow keeping the enemy's forward line from crossing into the sacred circle.

Hattie laid lines of warding stones and burned herbs whose smoke wound upward into spiraling, living walls while scolding the evil ones.

When the worst of the attack surged, they joined hands, pouring every shred of strength they had into a single act: raising a dome of shimmering green light over the grove. Roots below and branches above joined the spell, locking it in place.

The Sequoias continued to rain down their wisdom-Light in great, glittering waves on the enemies. And somewhere, far away, every ally in the ancient war felt it.

The ancient trees, older than any war, swayed without wind. Golden wisdom rained in hard sheets, burning away illusions, showing the enemy's rot for what it was.

Hattie and Beck fought the evil in the ring of ward-stones, their dome of Light trembling under the blows of iron and fire. Beck's axe sang. Hattie's chants wove tighter and tighter until the trees themselves began to answer—roots heaving up to tangle attackers, branches snapping down like the swing of a giant's arm.

The North Point — The Colorado Tower

Timmon's crew had barely finished turning the Folly to splinters when the next wave came. Smoke-dark shapes rolled across the plain, shape shifting into whatever the mind feared most. Timmon, Celia, Lou, Gordon, and Crazy Jack raced to the Tower.

The Tower bells pealed so hard the ground quivered. Celia fought at Timmon's side, blades flashing in arcs of light. Gordon and Lou threw spell after spell into the air, shattering the dark shapes before they could climb the Tower walls. Crazy Jack unleashed a mummery of verbiage cold enough to flash freeze the shadows.

East Point — The Shacky Cabin by the Sea

Shem felt it in his bones before he heard it—a deep, dragging roar from the water. The sound fled to the nearby town. The sea town's streets began to flood, not with ocean water but with something blacker and slower. Marisong stood at the shoreline, hair whipping, voice rising in a song that split the black tide in two. Geena's clay guardians—beasts, birds, and bowl-shaped shields—moved into place, holding the breach until the song could drive the darkness back.

South Point— The Desert Store

The chakra beneath the desert store pulsed hot, almost too hot to stand on. Cowboy Johnson, William, Lily, Emma, Eddy, and Normaine fought to keep the energy vortex clear.

Normaine's mobiles spun like bladed suns, cutting through anything that tried to cross the threshold. Eddy's hands flashed over every hinge, latch, and wheel, keeping the defenses moving faster than the enemy could react. Emma painted monsters on canvas after canvas, then splashed paint over them, obliterating them.

The Connection

At each of the five Points of Light, the warriors for Goodness began to feel the connection to each other. The rain of wisdom from the Sequoias fell over the Colorado plains, sharpening the Towers capacities. The Tower's new ringing sounds reached the sea, providing Marisong's magnetic sea songs new density. Her sea songs rolled south to the desert store, cooling the burning chakra the store sat on. And from the desert store, a wave of pure grounding rippled outward, steadying every hand and heart.

The enemy faltered. Not because they had been beaten in one place, but because they had been *seen, heard, and named* in all five places at once.

The Breaking Point

The enemy surged one last time. At each Point, the air split with high, needling shrieks—the sound of evil's minions trying to stitch themselves back together. Shadows poured into the Sequoias, boiled over the Colorado plains, rose in the black tide of the sea, and swarmed the desert store's threshold.

The Light answered.

West — The Sequoias

Hattie raised her arms, catching the golden rain in her palms. Beck's axe struck the ground, sending a shock wave through the roots, releasing them into movement. The Sequoias bent as one, their branches forming a living crown above the pair, and released every stored whisper of age and wisdom in a blazing pulse.

North — Colorado Tower

The Tower's bells hit a pitch they had never reached before—not loud, but *clear*. Celia's blades flashed in rhythm, cutting clean through the shapes. Timmon stepped forward and pounded the cane his father, Crowell Goforth Restus the Second, had given him into the ground; the ring of metal, magic, and chanting funeral rites from another world struck the evil. The earth rippled outward like a steel heartbeat. Crazy Jack filibustered, Gordon mimed to keep them off balance and Lou struck at them with deadly accuracy using her garden hoe.

East Point — The Sea

Marisong's voice rose until it was no longer human — it was sea, storm, and thunder rolled into one. The black tide of Shadows turned on itself, twisting into steam. Geena's clay guardians crumbled into dust that swirled into the air, sealing the breach in the horizon where the dark had come through. Shem and Miz Wind held hands and swung in a circle to magnetize any remnants of evil to the dirt under their feet where graves lay waiting for the Shadows.

South — The Desert Store

Avery Mott Judson, once nicknamed Cowboy Johnson, knelt and pressed his hands to the hot ground. At his touch, the chakra flared, shooting a column of light up through the earth.

Normaine's mobiles spun so fast they blurred into golden disks. Eddy's last adjustments locked the vortex in place, a gate that no shadow could cross. Emma threw paint into the air, and it spun into circles and collected shadows as it came down, burying them deep into the ground.

The Shattering

And then—all at once— every Point of Light pulsed. Five bursts, one heart.

The Shadows screamed, not from pain, but from *being seen.* Their secrets spilled into the open: the lies, the hunger, the rancid fears that drove them. Once named, they couldn't hold their dreadful shapes. They fractured, each breaking into a thousand specks of ash that rode the wind away.

Aftermath of the Battle

The world became still. At the West Point, the Sequoias no longer swayed in battle stance. Their branches hung low, shedding the last golden drops of wisdom like tears. Hattie leaned against Beck, her breath shallow but steady. Neither spoke. It was enough to know they'd stood between the oldest living things on earth and the teeth of the dark—and held.

In Colorado, the plains rolled out in silence toward where the Folly had once stood. The heap of boards, metal, and ruin was already losing its shape in the wind. Timmon stood at the Tower's base, Celia beside him, her blades tucked away. Gordon, Lou, and Crazy Jack were sitting down, gasping and resting.

"I say we're too damn old to keep doing this kind of stuff!" Gordon said. Lou and Crazy Jack nodded in agreement.

"Those two young people are going to have to do something about getting married and having babies to grow up to help them when we're gone!"

At the eastern sea, Marisong's voice had gone hoarse. She sat in the sand with the waves barely touching her feet, Shem, Miz Wind, Geena beside her, watching the clay dust drift on the wind toward the horizon. Somewhere out there, the sleeping women and men the sea held moved and smiled.

At the Desert Store, Avery—Cowboy Johnson— watched as the chakra's last shimmer of Light faded back into the earth. Normaine stood in the doorway, a mobile in her hands. Eddy, for once, didn't polish or adjust a thing.

The air was clean. Quiet. He wasn't in a hurry to break it. William and Lily Jean Bloome held hands and watched the Light settle back into its natural place. Emma sighed and wiped a painted hand across her face. War paint. She'd earned it!..

All five groups gathered their things after taking the needed time to recuperate before they headed to the desert store. The place where they had lived or been a part of its Goodness before. Except for Marisong and Miz Wind. They would never leave the sea. And Crazy Jack, who was intent on wooing a spinster in town.

They moved into the motel rooms and rested. The battle was over. The Dark Ones were gone—scattered and silenced by the Light. Avery Mott Judson stood once more at the center of the desert store's vortex, the oldest of the five Points of Light. Around him were gathered those who had fought beside him— each weary, each changed. For a time, they stayed there together, reliving old times and retracing old steps that led back to the odd gifts they each carried.

They cooked, talked, and mended what could be mended. Someone fixed coffee, someone swept sand from the doorway, someone made chili, someone built a fire, and laughter—fragile at first—began to rise again.

Their final gathering began slowly, like an old wagon easing into motion. Gordon stood first, stretching his back. "Lou and I are heading to my house," he said. "I happen to own one nearby. Beck, Hattie, would you two like to join us? The house and woods may have been misbehaving while I was gone."

Beck nodded without hesitation. "Somebody's got to keep the woods standing after what we just went through."

Hattie said, "I'll bake them sugar cookies! All that house needs is a good scolding!" She followed Gordon, Lou, and Beck out the door.

Timmon lingered, his eyes on Geena across the room. Celia had told him everything—about Ray, about the way Geena had been holding the place together with string and stubbornness. He walked over. "I'd like to go to Carolina with you for awhile," he drawled. "Maybe I can help."

Geena didn't answer right away, just studied his face as if weighing the offer against every disappointment she'd ever known. Finally, she nodded.

Shem said, "I'll be going back to Carolina. To the shore. To the sea. To Marisong. And Miz Wind." He added her name as an afterthought.

Emma asked Avery, "Would you like to go back to Spain with me for awhile? See Mama's beautiful resting place and meet your son?"

Avery nodded. Matthew rushed over.

"Can I go, too, Avery?"

Avery stared at him, emotions running across his face. Love, distaste, hurt and more…

The big giant of a man saw on Avery's face that the answer was no. He put his hands over his face and sobbed in big loud bellows.

"My father is crying. Who would have believed that was possible?" Avery murmured.

Perry, Susan, and Lana surrounded Avery. "We would like to go too, if that's okay, Avery."

Perry added. "And I will drive you by the prison of a house our father has faithfully kept those despicable murderers in all these years. There's a lot to do, Avery."

"Who will take care of the desert store?" Avery asked.

"Hector. He's going to keep an eye on things and report back to us. He knows what's going on"

"I should have known," Avery said.

"Okay. All of you. Let's go together."

They gathered around him and embraced each other.

Matthew shouted. "Don't leave me out! After all, he's my son!" and pushed into the group hug.

"Only if you buy the tickets, Matthew," Avery answered.

"Done!" Matthew shouted.

"Are you and Lily Jean Bloome coming with us?" Avery asked William the Dude.

"As soon as we get some things taken care of here," William answered. She nodded.

"How about you two, Normaine and Eddy? Want to go? Matthew's paying."

Matthew grimaced as though in pain, then grinned and nodded.

"Nope. You guys ain't going nowhere yet. There's stuff to be done first. We got a big show coming up in a couple months. Okay to take a bunch of the odd things we made for this war? They are pretty amazing. And, are there other things that need to be stored that we made? Like weapons? Dumbasses! This may happen again, you know. Me and Eddy are gonna' get a big rig and go to your war places and collect the needed things first. You all are going with us. Then you can leave. You all need to get the horse before the cart, dumbasses!"

Avery sobered. "The time away from here has taken its toll on me. I will be needing to see doctors about...things. I'm awfully tired in an odd way. There are things I must see to as soon as possible..."

His green eyes held a faraway look as though he was looking at something they would never see-or understand.

They all fell silent and began to change their answers. They would stick with Avery. Stand by him.

He looked at them and grinned slowly. "You go on about your business. I will call you if I need you."

They agreed. It was dusk. They drifted out to the new built campfire. Details tomorrow. Who rode with who and where and how to store things. One step at a time.

Normaine and Eddy roasted marshmallows. Hot dogs waited to be stuck on sticks and roasted. And bologna to be folded and fried on a stick. Cold beer, too. Pepperidge Farm triple chocolate cake in the freezer for dessert. They were home again. Misfits. Desert children. Lost but strong. The back door swung shut on the Desert Store. Laughter traced itself across the faces of all the misfits. They had won…this time.

The evil ones stayed silent for the time being. But they weren't done…

The End

Some things never end. Not the fight between Goodness and Evil. Somewhere between each wounded warrior and sometimes the silly warriors the Clown of All produces, lie others waiting to take the stage and fight the good fight.

Author's Note

This is the seventh book in the *Desert Store Series*; a collection of creative non-fiction stories rooted in my own life experience and those of others I've known. I've borrowed imagination where needed—but the core truths remain. This series speaks to the higher purposes we each encounter when we come together. Each book in the Desert Store Series is gritty, real, ridiculously humorous and raw—with touches of magic and redemption.

Writing this series has been a personal experience, a purging of things needing a voice.

I know others who have fought their way toward the Light and Love. If you are one of them, just know that in this series, the love never ends.

And so, the seven books in the *Desert Store Series* are all part truth, part imagination, and entirely soul. The genre is creative non-fiction. Drawn from my life experiences and inspired by others who've sidestepped struggles by being creative, this series aims at the best in each character in this series.

If you've lived and kept on going, this series is for you, dear reader. I hope that each characters story brings you light and humor, and the reminder that love—real love—never ends.